Prime

Real Estate

Sinful Grace

G&T Publishing

ISBN-1:
Prime Real Estate
Copyright © 2021 by G&T Publishing.

Dear Reader,

This book is a special book to me. It is the first LBGT standalone romance I wrote over a decade ago. It has been tweaked since then, but the storyline is the same. This edition comes with new edits and new cover art. I hope you all enjoy and let me know your thoughts.

I would like to dedicate this book to my friends. Without all the friends I have had over my lifetime so far, I would not have had the courage to do some of the things I have pushed myself to do, and I thank you.

As a married mother of four, life can become hectic. Nothing in life is worth doing if you are not passionate about it, and writing is a passion of mine.

There is a sweetness to this book that I have been told leaves you in a lull of satisfaction when completed. I hope you feel the same.

Always stay safe, my readers. You are all important. If you wish to check out more of my work, contact me, or provide feedback, please visit:

www.gt-publishing.com
https://www.facebook.com/SinfulGraceRomanceAuthor/
https://www.facebook.com/sinful.grace.romance
Chapters Interactive App: Sinful Grace
Twitter: @Sinful_Grace
Instagram: @Sinful_Grace
Remember,
You can't have history without a story in it!

Sinful Grace

Just because love is lost,
Does not mean one is broken.

Chapter 1

"Alright, that's the last of them. I'll be taking those with me, though."

Pointing to the two bags of luggage piled at the screen door, she made sure nothing would be left behind. Forming in the pit of her stomach. With every step, the ache intensified, becoming almost unbearable as she walked into the doorway of what was *their* bedroom.

Natalia squashed it to the back of her mind, but not before a flashback of Dan walking towards her with tears running down her cheeks invaded her thoughts. Letting out a heavy sigh, she turned around and collided with Rachel.

"I'm so sorry I didn't see you standing there."

Frowning, Rachel rubbed at her shoulder.

"Are you still sure you want to go through with this?" She asked pointedly. "I mean -I- I can see that this is hard for you, and you're tearing yourself up inside." Blowing out a sigh, "I just don't want you to regret anything."

Gently placing a hand on her friend's shoulder, she gave a tight nod. Rachel always could read her better than anyone else. She agreed it was a fast-made decision to move, but she knew in her heart it was the right choice.

Having already gone through all the details, she could feel that her friend needed the reassurance.

Not in the right state of mind to go back through it all, she swallowed, fighting the urge to crumble apart. Pushing herself through all the turmoil - as Dan had done - was proving challenging.

"We have been through this," Natalia responded with a roll of her eyes. "Yes, I'm sure it is the right thing to do, and you know very well why," she bit out. "I can't be around all the memories."

A shiver of embarrassment spread as her voice cracked, and she cleared her throat. "Besides, I have been talking about taking a break for a while now. This just gave me the *oomph* to go ahead with it."

Natalia gestured her lack of caring with her outstretched arm. Turquoise eyes narrowed as Rachel shook her dirty blonde head at her. The motion always reminded Natalia of wild rice, bringing a small quirk to her lips.

"Don't look at me like that. You know better than anyone why I'm doing all of this."

Straightening, she released a long breath of air, Natalia took the slight reprieve to collect her thoughts. Coming in only two inches shorter than her at 5'2, Rachel could still make anyone feel tiny under her scrutiny.

"You're right. I do understand why you need to get away, but I still think this is a little much." Groaning her words, "I mean, when you talked about getting away, I didn't think you meant an early retirement."

Pinching the bridge of her nose to starve off the building headache, she closed her eyes.

"Not only are your clients going to be upset, but I'm gonna miss you like crazy."

Her hand fell to her side, and her eyes popped open.

"You'd better call me as soon as you get there. You know you can't buy a house without my approval. I insist you call me when you are sure you found the diamond in the rough."

Her words blurred together in a rush, and Natalia almost didn't understand the jumbled mess.

"You know I will. Besides, I must ensure my maid will be comfortable in her quarters."

Plastering on a giant smile, Natalia took a step back, eyes wide, acting as though she was offended.

"Oh, don't give me that look. You know the minute you come to visit, you'll be picking things up and cleaning. I could never have you as a regular guest." Rachel smiled and relaxed.

Nodding her head, Natalia maneuvered past her, making her way down the empty hall. The old musty smell of dust and oak always reminded her of Dan. Resigned, Natalia took one more languid look around.

All the possibilities that could've been made her pause slightly as she turned to get her bags. Rachel, shaking her head, picked up the luggage and started for the door. Pushing her emotions aside, Natalia rushed past her and opened the door with a wink. Her reward was a smile.

With odd grunting noises, Rachel hauled the luggage into the trunk. Despondently, Natalia picked up the small package through the passenger side window and slowly made her way down to the mailbox.

Kissing the package goodbye, it slipped out of her fingers and into the metal box. A sigh escaped her lips. A sign of her letting go of the past and things she couldn't change and a promise for better things to come.

On her way back to the SUV, with lines of mud and dust marks thick enough to draw pictures, a sense of accomplishment washed over her.

You can do this.

Leaning against the driver's side door, Rachel stared at the ground. As she approached, her head lifted, revealing a flushed face and red-rimmed eyes. Natalia gathered her friend in her arms.

"It'll be okay, I promise," she squeezed. "You never know, maybe you'll want to come and move in with me,"

A small chuckle and another squeeze. Natalia's attempt to make light of the situation.

Rachel pulled away to wipe her eyes. It tore at her heart to see her friend like this. The forced smile doing nothing to disguise her true emotions. The soft sniffles, rosy cheeks, bloodshot eyes, and tears that made her mascara leave spider-like lines had her heart squeezing forcibly in her chest.

You're even more beautiful when you're a mess.

"I am going to miss you like crazy. Wherever you end up, you better be happy, or you're coming back to stay with me." She said, straightening herself.

"I mean it. Now go ahead and go before I get all emotional again and beg you to stay."

She never thought she could care for her friend any more than she already did, but in that instant, she could feel her heart swelling more. Taking Rachel in her arms for a big bear hug, she assured her she'd call when she figured out where she was staying.

This chapter of her life ending, with the echo of the car door closing. Effusive feelings of tumultuous emotions filled her throat, threatening to choke her and causing her to doubt her decision. Wavering a bit, she pushed those thoughts from her mind. Never had she been through so much that it had her changing the course of her life.

Life can be a twister in some ways. Swallowing things in its path, but where you drop to pick up the pieces could be even better than where you started from.

At least that's what I'm hoping for, she told herself.

Keys jingled as she started the car. Rachel stepped away, giving her room. With one last sad wave goodbye, Natalia rolled down the driveway. Glancing back in the rearview mirror silently, she wished herself luck in her future wherever it took her.

Chapter 2

Nick was just getting ready to go to lunch when her intercom buzzed. Reluctantly, she pushed down the button.

"Miss Ward, I have a car pulling up. Do you want me to tell them we are closed for lunch?"

Of course, someone was coming, mentally willing them to go away. It would have been the first day in a week that she would be able to take an hour off to enjoy some nice food with the sun shining through the clouds, but as always, it would have to wait. Waking back to reality, the intercom buzzed again.

"No Colleen, I'll take them. Show them back and put the closed lunch sign in the window before you go." Leaning forward in her seat, she stared down at the intercom. "Oh, and please remember, It's Nick."

After her receptionist mumbled her apologies, Nick got up from her desk to stare out the window. Colleen was a lovely woman, although forgetful at times. She hired the inexperienced 22-year-old when opening the agency over 3 years ago.

The quirky petite blonde was in desperate need of a job. Nick remembered how hard it was trying to break into the career world and figured if she could help, she would. So, she hired her.

The girl's flirty demeanor, light brown eyes, and beaming smile drew attention wherever she was.

Not attracted to her herself, Nick couldn't help but notice a lot of the men in town turning their heads to watch her as she passed.

A black Lexus Rx – that she did not recognize - rolled up and parked in the visitors' area. Living in a small town, she knew pretty much everyone, even if she's lived in Carlton for only nine years.

After graduating at 25 from Virginia State with a Bachelor's in Business and obtaining her real-estate license, Nick climbed into her old Jeep and drove until she ran out of money and gas. Breaking down in this old town was the best accident that had ever occurred to her. Content with herself and her life, Nick never looked back.

Who is that?

The slender brunette easing out of the SUV made her heart flutter. Even being too far away to see her face didn't stop the sudden anxious excitement filling her chest. The abruptness of it had her taken aback. Suddenly overwhelmed and self-conscious over meeting this woman, Nick swiveled around to check herself in the mirror.

Looking good, she thought to the woman reflecting back at her. Nonetheless, she straightened her silk purple shirt, wiped off her grey dress pants, and pulled back her strawberry blonde hair into a clip.

Nodding, Nick strode back to her desk. Fidgeting, she took a few calming breaths and waited for her visitor.

When the knock sounded on the door, she called out for them to enter. Her receptionist's familiar light brown eyes greeted her as they stepped in and, with a sweep of her arm, motioned for their guest to enter. Taking note of the wink Colleen gave her, she rolled her eyes at the closing of the door.

The creature that just walked through the mahogany door filled her mind with one word.

Stunning.

At first glance, the woman's eyes looked pitch black, but walking closer to shake her hand, she noticed tiny specs of gold sprinkled in.

A starry night sky.

The hand she held was warm and soft, sending small prickles up her arm. A small voice coaxed through her fog of a brain, but Nick was unable to fully register what it said.

Realizing she was staring, Nick quickly diverted her eyes to her desk. Pulling her hand back, she shouted for Colleen to have a nice lunch while waving her hand for the woman to come and have a seat. Instinctively, Nick rolled her eyes again when Colleen mumbled something on the other side of the door before leaving them in silence.

ༀ

She could have come back later, she told the receptionist, noticing the 'out for lunch' sign being placed in the window. With a smile, she reassured her it was okay. The need to not be a burden had her reminding herself that this was their job, and she dampened the anxiety and anticipation that tried to rise up.

Remembering how to get to this town wasn't the hard part - trying to find a realtor to talk to was. Stopping for gas earlier, after her phone died, she had struck up a conversation with the gas station attendant.

He suggested she talk to Nick Ward and briefly gave her directions with a phone number. The number was of no use to her with a dead phone. Something she was guilty of a lot. Unsure if she was in the right place, she double-checked the directions against the sign out front of the tan Victorian reading Ward Realty.

The building was homey. Vintage wallpaper and modern décor outfitted it nicely. The cherry and bubbly receptionist who greeted her when she stepped inside eased her newcomer nerves a bit. Explaining that they could still help her, she started to feel like she could relax. That is – until she stepped into the office.

Surprised to see a woman sitting behind the desk, Natalia's spine stiffened a bit. From the last name and the way the gas station attendant spoke, Natalia thought she would be meeting with a man.

Tingles ran up her arm as she shook the woman's outstretched hand. Her palm cool against her clammy one. A hint of vanilla registered when she took her hand back. Instantly, her skin chilled at the loss of contact.

Heat rose to her cheeks, meeting the woman's intense stare. Not usually the center of attention, Natalia didn't quite know what else to do but stare right back. Those glittering green eyes got darker just before the other woman broke the contact to focus on her desk.

Thrown off guard, Natalia completely missed the gesture for her to sit. Blushing again, she realized the woman was waiting for her to take the seat in front of the desk.

What is it with this woman? Pondering to herself. *Get a grip*, she chided for her lack of control over her libido.

Taking a seat, "I'm sorry, but I was told to come and speak with Nick. If he is out, I can come back at another time."

The woman's smile started to turn into a mild frown. Natalia didn't mean to offend her. She could see from the plaques in her office that she was good at whatever she did.

Moments of silence passed, making her feel uncomfortable. Contemplating if she should stay, Natalia gripped the armrest, about to get up when the woman spoke.

"I am Nick." She stated, running her hand down her purple shirt, "Nicole Ward, to be exact. Everyone knows me as Nick, though. I'm guessing you need a realtor Miss...?"

"Purez. Natalia Purez." She responded, straightening herself. "And yes, I require a realtor."

Natalia let out a nervous laugh, "I am so sorry, I just expected to see a man when the guy at the gas station told me to go and talk to Nick. He never mentioned one way or the other if you were a woman or a man."

This woman has me tripping all over myself. Shut up and pay attention, Nat.

Her words spilled out. "Serves me right for assuming."

Lifting her hand, she wiped a stray hair from her shoulder. Natalia looked around the room some more. There – on the desk – sat a plaque, and in silver letters spelled out 'Nick Ward.'

Well, there you go. I put my foot in my mouth again.

This prompted her to take a closer look at the pictures on the wall. All of them were of Nick with, whom Natalia assumed to be friends or clients. Flooded with embarrassment, Natalia cleared her throat and turned her attention back to Nick.

Smiling, Nick relaxed back into her chair. Natalia followed in response, hoping this appointment wasn't a lost cause.

"So, what exactly brought you out to Carolton, Mississippi, Natalia?"

Natalia couldn't help but notice the long sturdy fingers as they grasped a pen nearby. Wondering what those fingers would feel like brushing against her bare skin had her letting go of a shiver.

Where did that come from?

Glancing up, she was relieved Nick hadn't noticed. While Nick was busy searching her desk, Natalia attempted to steady her beating heart with a few deep breaths. Recovering herself, she cleared her throat. Bringing the attention back to herself, a rush of heat crept up her body.

Placing down a pad of paper, Nick's eyes trailed over her. Her mouth ran dry at the obvious inspection. Appreciating her view, Natalia focused on those full lips. Natalia watched her throat shift as she swallowed. Feeling her body warming, Natalia clasped her hands in her lap.

"Well, my grandmother used to live out this way." Ignoring the slight rise in her tone, she continued, "and my father used to bring me up here every other summer for a week to spend during break. I've always loved the charm of the old houses."

Pressing her back firmly against the chair, she took a deep breath to calm her nerves. When she felt confident enough that she wouldn't squeak as she spoke, she continued.

"It's so much different from the dusty terrain of Tennessee. Recently," she shifted in her seat, 'I sold my veterinary practice to take an early retirement. I need time to wind down and enjoy life. I figured Carolton was the closest thing to feeling like home for me."

A shaky breath escaped her lips, and perspiration beaded her lip as more heat crept up her neck. Nick had stopped writing and was - once again - staring at her.

"Ummm, is there something wrong, Miss Ward?" Her voice laced with concern.

"N-no."

She responded with a smile and a shake of her head.

"I mean, no. It's just… I've sold a lot of property, and I haven't heard anyone talk about this town - that way - in such a long time. It's kind of refreshing."

Stopping to jot down some more notes, Nick peered back at her.

"So, what exactly are you looking for in a property? How much are you willing to spend?"

Chapter 3

For some reason, it was difficult to concentrate on what Natalia was saying. Nick hadn't had this much trouble with her wild thoughts,

More like erotic…

- in a couple of years, but trying to keep her mind from wandering was becoming very rigorous. The tan skin and fluttering eyes captured her attention and like a flower to the sun, she was pulled toward her.

Hearing Miss Purez was from Tennessee surprised her. She expected to see a rough, worn-down cowgirl, but instead, what was sitting across from her was soft, tan skin and divine legs. Wandering eyes rested on supple lips. Lips her tongue craved to taste. A muffled noise broke through her daze.

"I'm sorry," shaking her head, "I missed half of that. I seem to be having trouble concentrating this afternoon."

"It's ok. Where did you want to start?"

Oh… there are so many places.

Subtly sliding her sweaty hands down her back pockets, Nick hoped Natalia didn't notice.

"Do you mind if I just ask you a couple of questions? It'll help me narrow down what you want."

Those full lips gave Nick too many ideas and she found herself having to peel her eyes away.

Brushing something off of her dark brown khaki shorts, Natalia sat straight up in her seat.

"Well," she began, "I am looking for an older home. It doesn't have to be completely updated, as long as there are no major repairs needed to be done."

A hint of anxiety as her pitch rose. Leaving a mental note in the back of her mind, Nick thought of all the options that would ease her mind.

"I don't want to worry about a roof or other structural repairs."

Natalia wrung her hands together in her lap after pushing back an invisible strand of hair.

"Preferably a minimum of three bedrooms. I would like a place with some land. Maybe already with a barn?"

Natalia paused and furrowed her brow. Giving her time, Nick added this information to her notes. It would help narrow down the search later.

"I would eventually like to start a little farm of my own," she continued. Stopping her note-taking. Lifting her eyes, Nick caught her breath at the shimmering brightness of her eyes.

"I would need room enough for a barn and maybe some large animals."

Collecting herself, Nick dropped her eyes back down to her open notes, jotting down more.

"I might even start a small practice out of my home, so the potential for an office or maybe even rental income as well."

"Do you have a price range you are working from?" Nick inquired, scribbling more notes onto her notepad.

"I have a good amount stocked away from selling my practice and funds my family left me,"

Natalia mentioned as she worked her neck from side to side.

Memorized, Nick's eyes traveled with her movements. The low cracking noises elicited soft moans from the woman sitting across from her.

"So," coughing to clear her throat, "money shouldn't be a problem, as long as we don't go crazy."

Arching an eyebrow, she repressed the automatic sigh that wanted to escape. Nick knew most of her clients, at the very least, had a ceiling. Natalia straightened in her seat, and with a smile, she broke the silence.

"Ideally,"

Here we go,

"I would like to go no more than $400,000, and that is with repairs."

There it is.

Nick smirked and made another note.

"I will be paying mostly in cash or certified bank check, so I would assume sellers would be more willing to work with price."

Nick agreed with a nod.

"Most importantly, I want something that feels like home."

Again, she rubbed her hands on her shorts. Her nervousness evident but Nick didn't understand why. When she first strolled into her office, she radiated confidence.

Finishing up her notes, Nick set her pad and pen aside. Leaning forward, hands folded and a slight tilt to her lips, she broke the silence.

"Now that we have all of that settled Mrs. Purez, I will compile a list together of some properties for you to look at tomorrow."

An awkward moment of quiet passed where their eyes locked on each other, only for Natalia to glance toward the notepad on the desk.

Nick cleared her throat, "Unless you are dead set on looking today."

The woman in front of her was, for lack of a better word, mesmerizing. Several times she forced herself to re-focus on the task at hand.

With a voice similar to silk, "Oh no, it's okay. We can go tomorrow."

An ache grew in the pit of her stomach, catching herself before she ran a finger across the bottom lip Natalia suckled on. Nick's attention trained on the plump pink lip.

"I have to find a place to stay," Natalia continued, causing Nick to hastily raise her gaze.

Get a grip, inanely criticizing herself.

"Until I find a house anyway," Natalia giggled. "And I'm starving."

Me too.

"I haven't eaten since I got here, and I don't think my stomach would be too happy with me if I don't do its bidding soon." A smile stretched from ear to ear. "So, do you want to go grab some lunch?"

Puzzled, Nick looked at her watch. "I'm sorry I don't think I caught that last part."

Looking her straight in the eyes, Nick crossed her legs and rubbed her hands together on the desk.

Get it together, Nick. Stop acting like a teenager.

"I thought that since you were having trouble concentrating, it might be because you haven't eaten lunch either."

Natalia quickly went on, "I mean I'm presuming that you haven't since you were just placing the sign in the window when I came in. Since I'm new in town, maybe you had a decent place in mind to grab a bite."

Her inability to rip her eyes away from Natalia caused more problems, including the building of electricity between both women. The increasing heartbeat made her jittery, to the point of wanting to jump out of her seat. Never liked being looked at, Nick always had problems with social situations. It was one of the reasons she almost flunked debate class.

"Unless you had something else you were planning to do?" Natalia's voice rose an octave. "I - I don't mean to intrude. I just - I thought… Oh, I'm so sorry I'm mumbling."

Nick recognized Natalia's embarrassment from the apparent blush rising up her neck and settling in her cheeks. The pull to kiss her took Nick by surprise, and abruptly, she pushed her seat back, stood, and wiped her sweaty palms onto the back of her pants. Needing the extra seconds to recover, she cleared her throat again before she gave into her inner need to lean over the desk and cover the other woman's mouth with her own.

"I don't have anything else planned for lunch. If you'd like, I could show you to this nice little deli shop right in town. They have great sandwiches, and I am famished."

Ending with a wink, Nick was rewarded with a radiant smile.

Yeah, she thought, *I'm hungry, all right, but it isn't for anything outside of this room.*

A low growl emanating from her stomach drowned out her thoughts.

"I also know of a place you could stay and it's not far from there."

Natalia's smile felt like a pat on the head, causing satisfying tingles all over her.

Slow down, Nick. She just got here. You're acting like she's a shiny new toy to play with.

Nodding, Natalia stood, brushing herself off. A little shorter than her 5'7, Natalia is the perfect height and all-woman. Casually, she looked her up and down but realized that she wasn't as graceful as she thought.

Natalia's neck curiously bloomed a light pink again. Shifting her eyes, she caught the other woman snapping her focus away from her.

Was she checking me out?

No... no. Maybe?

Not wasting any more time, Nick motioned toward the door. Clicking the lock in place, Nick instructed Natalia to follow her. Once they were both in their vehicles, Nick chided herself for staring earlier. She was not as young as she used to be and this wasn't some high school crush. Reminding herself several times that she's a client and things need to remain professional.

But, her mind chimed in, which she ignored by checking the rear-view mirror, starting her car, and backing out onto the main road for town. The whole drive, Nick tried to keep her thoughts PG. With her mind racing and her hands itching to touch, Nick gripped the steering wheel tight, causing her knuckles to turn white.

Yup, I'm in trouble.

∽

Wow. I am stuffed.

Natalia's turkey sandwich was nothing like the ones back home. Packed full of meat, that first bite was intimidating. Barley able to open her mouth wide enough. She was proud of herself for finishing the whole thing. The company wasn't bad at all, either.

When she first got out of her truck, Nick had seemed a little distant. Nick followed a hostess who sat them at a booth viewing the parking lot. After ordering, Nick eased back into her seat.

"Glad you liked it," Nick's voice muffled by a mouthful of food. It didn't seem to be hard for her to concentrate at lunch. Nick asked tons of questions. Some Natalia answered easily, while others she shied away from. There were particular things she wasn't prepared to talk about.

When Nick wondered if she was seeing anyone, Natalia shrugged in response. Nick dropped the subject. Grateful she didn't push it, but Nick was talkative.

The other woman entertained her with stories of rolling into town. The animated hand movements and embarrassing scenarios had Natalia laughing loudly, and the waitress came over to inquire if she was OK. Behind teary eyes, they noticed other patrons staring. That only served to make them laugh harder.

Catching Nick looking at her several times sent shivers down her spine. Deep green eyes darkened, making her skin flush. When it happened, Nick quickly looked away.

Seeing a fire blaze behind Nick's eyes, then suddenly dimming, like the pilot light on a gas

23

fireplace, had Natalia feeling a mix of sympathy and surprise. Natalia had a sense of admiration for Nick. Other than these moments, she was nothing but composed the entire time.

At times, Nick would start to talk about her past only to stop mid-sentence, leaving a sullen expression on her face. Natalia ached inside to think that this beautiful creature had been hurt so badly at one point in life.

Shifting to the happenings in town, Nick's face would come alive. Her eyes would light up, and her voice would crack with emotion. The stress would melt away from her face.

The few moments of laughter during their conversation brought Natalia's spirits up. The few times she made her laugh, it echoed throughout her entire body and made her feel like she could do anything. Natalia never wanted that sound to end.

Wrapping up their lunch and splitting the bill, she followed Nick across the street to the Wicker B&B down a few buildings. After parking her car, Nick walked her down the pathway, almost to the front steps, and extended her hand. Disappointed to have their time end, Natalia shook it, knowing the other woman had to get back to work.

Casualty mentioning she would be in touch, Nick turned, leaving her to watch Nick's backside sway as she strutted away down the sidewalk.

She has a nice ass.

Appreciating how those slacks conformed to her bottom. Images played in her mind as she gazed after her. Blinking rapidly to regain her composure, Natalia turned towards the building.

This is the B&B?

The beautifully detailed wrap-around porch overshadowed the sign out front. Green grass shimmered against the white wood. The yellow farmhouse, with its age starting to show around the windows, was a stark contrast to the opposite side of the quiet main street. Small brick storefronts lined the tree-spotted road. Somehow, with no more than ten buildings lining the two-way street, this town seemed to buzz.

"You can do this," A steady breath escaping her lips had her chest rising and falling before she took the steps up the front porch.

"This was the right move," she encouraged herself. The foyer of the old building emits peacefulness from the honey-colored walls to the warm oak floor.

At one point in time, she bet a bunch of rugrats roamed the now quiet hallways. Striding up to the front desk, where an elderly woman no older than seventy sat knitting a multicolored blanket.

She greeted, "Hello." Smiling so wide, her face hurt. "I am looking for a room. Do you have anything available?"

The woman stopped knitting. Her face pulled back with a grin, hinting at her once-flawless skin. It reminded Natalia of her grandmamma before she passed away.

"Sure do, darling!"

The woman paused her knitting.

"How long are you looking to stay?"

Leaning over the counter, she gave her a once over, "You look a bit familiar. Have I seen you before?"

Natalia crossed her arms and cleared her throat. Trying not to frown, the need to chew her nails gaining momentum, she responded.

"Maybe you have. I used to come up here with my dad to visit my grandmother a few times." Voice cracking with emotion.

"She passed away a few years ago."

The heartache climbing up her throat had her letting out a light cough.

"That's been a long time ago now, though. I used to love coming up here. That's why I'm trying to buy a piece of it now."

You could tell the very moment that her mind clicked. The elderly woman's eyes lit up with excitement.

"Oh! Your Mayz's little firecracker! She used to talk about you all the time! She would tell everyone at least a month before you'd be coming."

The chair creaked as she moved to the edge.

"She always seemed so much happier when you were around. You gave her so much to look forward to." Lowering her voice, a solemn calmness ensued as the woman patted Natalia's hand on the counter. "Sorry for your loss."

Natalia just nodded as the woman continued, "So you're looking to move into our quaint town?"

She beamed and smacked a hand on the desk.

"Well, I can't say I blame you. I love it here, although every now and then we get some city folk, but they can only stand the peace and quiet for so long." She scoffed.

"Silence always sends them packing and moving back to all the noise." She emphasized with a wave of her arm.

Pushing that topic aside, she rushed on. "So, I'm gonna guess you'll be here for a lil' while till you find something. I'll give you one of the suites, so you're a bit more comfortable."

Natalia opened her mouth and was quelled by a shush.

"No reason to say no. Mayz would have it no other way."

"Oh, I couldn't ask you to do that. What if you need it?"

"Pish posh. We won't need it." She dismissed her concerns with a flick of her wrist, "Besides, I have other rooms available. Now let me get you the keys so you can unpack. I'll have dinner ready in the dining room in about…" She glanced at the clock on the wall, "two hours if you'd like to join us."

Grabbing the room key, the woman came from behind the counter and pulled Natalia into a big hug.

"Welcome to Mississippi." Her voice sang. Releasing her, she took a step back. With a warm smile, she squeezed her shoulders.

"By the way, I'm Gracie. If you need anything, just let me know." She said, letting go and handing her a key. "Now go get your things. Your room is on the second floor in the corner. You'll love the view."

Turning, Gracie went back behind the counter, where she scribbled something in a book prior to returning to her knitting. Bewildered, Natalia walked outside to her SUV. Shading her eyes from the falling sun, she pulled her luggage out of the trunk. The rolling bag landed on the ground with a thud. Her back already sore from the long drive.

Usually, she wouldn't have packed so much, but this was a move, not a vacation. Sighing, she got out her duffle bag and closed the trunk, leaving the rest of her bags in the car for now.

On the way to her room, images of soft lips and dark green luring eyes played with her vision. Dampness built between her thighs, causing her cheeks to get warm.

"Damn it. Why can't I control myself?" Chiding herself.

Slowly shaking her head, still unable to completely erase the images. "It's only the first day… She's probably not even a lesbian, so why am I bothering with thinking about it."

As if echoing her thoughts would change the fact that she was starting to feel something. For now, Natalia pushed the comments to the back of her mind. She had other pressing matters to worry about.

Opening the door, Natalia was stunned by the view. Gracie had been telling the truth. She loved it. The room was a glow with the curtains pulled back to expose the evening sun falling over lush green hills.

A glittering lake sat about an acre back from the house, with geese littering the surface. Weeping willows sat along the edge, with flowers just beginning to bloom. It was the most peaceful thing she had seen in months. Heck, maybe even years.

Opening the sliding door to the balcony, Natalia stepped out. Air swirled around her, sliding her hair to the side. Sucking in a long breath, she released it with a 'whoosh.' A tiny squirrel that had been perched on the railing jumped and ran down the side.

Chapter 4

This time of the year, Carolton was just starting to see vacationers. Carolton always had a spark of electricity, a newness to everything, just like when she would visit as a girl, but now it seemed less crowded. Had Carolton changed that much since she had been here last? The early summer breeze stroked her face in a soft caress as she inhaled the scent of dew and earth.

Finally prying herself away from the balcony, Natalia decided a nice long shower was in order. While rinsing her body off, her mind floated back to thoughts of Nick again.

Unbidden, unhindered images of Nick's naked body, beads of water trickling down her pale skin, made her moan. Picturing full breast glimmering and Nick's back arching from the pressure of the water against her bare skin.

Natalia slammed her eyes shut at the warm tingly sensation roaming from her stomach and resting between her thighs. With ease, fingers slid into the folds between her legs to find that she was soaked. She imagined how Nick's nipples would harden at her touch, how they would taste as she suckled them into her mouth.

The entire time she thought about Nick, the slickness between her legs got worse. Not wanting to miss dinner, Natalia envisioned Nick's body once more, bringing herself to climax.

Panting, she went limp against the shower wall. "You sure do got it bad, girl. This is no way to break in the neighbors," she murmured to the emptiness.

Sated, Natalia finished washing herself off and toweled dry. In the bedroom, she threw open her suitcase, staring at her folded clothes. Pulling on a lace bra and panties, Natalia decided not to go back out tonight.

Instead, she threw on her red flannel pajama pants with a matching tank, grabbed her black hair clip, and twisted her hair up to secure it in place. A wave of exhaustion hit her, relaxing her muscles.

Too tired to even think about food, she tossed her bags onto the floor and crawled into bed, not even bothering to close the balcony doors or fold down the blankets. The summer breeze swept over her face as sleep claimed her.

∽

Slowly, with every step she took, Natalia began to undress. Drinking in the way her fingers peeled back the buttons on her white shirt before it fell to the floor. A low moan escaped as her hands snaked down to do the same to her khaki shorts.

Every exposure of skin had Nick's mouthwatering, her hands craving to pull her to her, and her heart racing. With a flick of her legs, Natalia's white *Nikes* flew off and landed on the floor by the closet. Soft words of seduction milked more need out of her, and Nick leaned back on her elbows, waiting to pounce.

Natalia finished undressing and took the last few steps toward her. With every swish of her hips, Nick pulsed between her needy thighs. Dry lips being wet in anticipation and hands sweaty with the need to touch her.

Reaching the bed, she crawled on. Natalia covered and began to undress her. Every once in a while, soft hands brushed her skin with a petting sensation.

I can't believe how tender she is. Maybe she had been waiting forever to be near me too, Nick said to herself.

Natalia claimed her mouth, her fingers plunging into Nick's wet folds. Nick screamed. Pleasure ripping through her body. Natalia worked her finger in and out of her. Her need covered her hand, and after only a few strokes, Nick screamed out again in ecstasy, only to wake up and realize that she had climaxed.

Jolting awake, Nick couldn't believe she climaxed in her sleep. Breathing heavily, her hands slide between her legs, feeling the evidence. The erotic images were increasingly vivid, and she awoke with a start.

Expecting to still see those dreamy star-like eyes. Blinking to clear the fogginess left her feeling a bit dazed and lonely. Having been a long time since dating another woman, let alone having anyone in her bed.

Nick rested back on her pillow, missing the warmth and comfort the dream had given her. Only focusing on work left little time for anything else.

Pulling in clients and making a name for herself in such a small area wasn't easy. All the money she made and awards she had won over the years sustained her need to excel but only deepened her need for companionship.

Still unable to believe that after only one meeting, Nick fought back the need to be near her and touch her. Nick's reaction to the other woman had her both self-conscious and longing for more.

She lay on her back, and slowly, her breathing started to calm down. Her body was hot, and Nick knew she was flush. If her sheets weren't damp, she could deny it. Sighing, she pulled the covers almost to her chin and pushed her head into her pillow, replaying the dream again.

"I always do this to myself."

The fabric muffling the words. Groaning, she lifted her head.

What is wrong with me?

"I need to get a pet or something. They're much more controllable and reliable than females," she blurted to the dark room.

In an effort to clear her head, Nick forced the thoughts to the back of her mind. It wasn't an easy task. When her mind latched onto something, it usually stuck. After tossing and turning for about an hour, her mind and body shut down enough that she drifted into a deep sleep once again.

Chapter 5

Waking up to the sound of "Unbreak My Heart" by Toni Braxton, Natalia realized it was her cell phone. Grunting, she pried herself from bed, only to fall back down onto it. Her right leg was numb from not moving all night, causing pain to run up the length of her leg as blood rushed through her veins.

As fast as she could, Natalia sprung up and hopped herself over to her suitcase. The ringing subsided just as she pulled out her phone. Grumbling to herself over not recognizing the number, she pressed call back in case it was Nick trying to reach her.

After the third ring, she was about to hang up when a female answered.

"Hello," she said. Not hiding her irritation. "Did someone try to call Natalia?"

Sniffling filled the silence. Then, a cough. "Hi, Nat, it's me."

A drawn-out Pausing had Natalia's mind racing.

"How could you just pack up and leave without even a word? I can't believe how selfish your being." The sniffling was followed by a blow of the nose.

At first, Natalia was going to say the woman had the wrong number, but taking stock of the sullen voice on the other end, irritation filled her.

"Selfish? Me, selfish! How dare you." She hissed.

Another blow of the nose, "Nat – "

"You're the one who threw away what we had. You not only walked out on me for a man, but you were heartless when you expected me to take you back and care for the child you conceived with him. Dan..." Her voice broke as she said the other woman's name.

Great, now I am crying.

Furious at herself for letting this woman get to her again, Natalia tried to push past the hurt and anger to no avail.

"I don't know what you expect from me?" Gritting her teeth, she wiped her eyes. "I loved you with everything I had. I gave up so much for you only to have it thrown back in my face."

Rage set in, and she breathed harshly into the phone. Attempting to calm herself, she focused on slowing her breathing.

I am not giving her the satisfaction of hearing me cry again.

The big huge huff of air on the other end was proof that Dan was trying to regain control of herself too.

"I wanted you. I...I tried, but you were never around. So, I found someone who would be."

The exasperated tone and the way she played the victim had the hair prickling on the back of her neck.

"I was sorely mistaken."

A second of silence filled the line.

"And I admit it. I loved you and still do."

Natalia rolled her eyes at that lie.

You don't cheat and ruin relationships when you love someone, she wanted to retort but stayed silent while Dan continued with her speech.

"That never changed. The way you handle things is absurd," Dan's tongue lashed out.

"Running away like this when I needed someone. You weren't there, once again. Rick was, though."

Contempt spilled from her voice. She wanted something and it wasn't going her way.

"He is very good at consoling, comforting, and everything you weren't capable of. I was, once again reminded of why I went to him in the first place."

Natalia heard her blow her nose once more. The muffled noise filled her ear.

"Now I will have the family I never could have had if I had stayed with you."

There it was. The words Dan has been dying to utter. Natalia imagined her proud of herself. Dan's mood changed so rapidly; it gave Natalia whiplash.

Wasn't she just whining about loving her?

Playing the victim once again, Dan was mad at her, focusing on why she cheated and made it her fault.

Typical manipulative Dan.

"I'm glad for you." Her words were ungenuine and cold. "You found something you wouldn't have found with me. Full control of a household."

It was her turn to let loose and get what she was feeling out.

"You didn't like that we had to work together to be a couple, and I didn't bend to your every word."

Bottled in irritation, grief and sadness boiled up. Memories full of painful moments sprinkled into her vision and left her feeling sour. Every word was bitten out as though she had eaten into a rotten apple.

"I see you found yourself a new puppet to do it for you. Although, I feel kind of sorry for him. Even more so for that baby that's growing inside you."

Natalia sucked in a deep breath and held it for a few seconds before slowly releasing it. The petty comment had the weight on her chest, easing a bit. Suddenly, she heard what sounded like a muffled growl on the other end.

"I hope you treat it well. That baby only deserves the best." Her words sincere. "As for me leaving, I did what was best for me. You have no say in what I do anymore."

A long sigh released, and hot tears warmed her cheeks. Her anger dissipated as they slowly slid down.

"So why did you call me Dan?" Natalia pinched her nose between her fingers. "Just to rub in that you were back with Rick? Or to try and make me feel sorry for leaving?"

Finally, the tears stopped long enough to regain her composure. Mentally jarring herself, she straightened her back and squared her shoulders. Noting how much easier it is to talk to her when she couldn't see her face.

Dan expelled another rumble. "I just wanted an explanation! I couldn't understand why you decided to leave without even consulting me!"

Natalia visualized the waving of the arms Dan usually did when she wasn't getting her way.

"Frankly, it was very rude to do after everything."

Yea, after everything, Natalia thought with another roll of her eyes.

"Just to throw away seven years. Seven years Nat! Seems a little silly. I came back to you to at least give it a try, and once again, you weren't there for me."

Natalia shook her head, visualizing the disgusted look on Dan's face.

She wasn't serious, was she? Dan was delusional if she thought this would work.

"Just packing it all up and walking away seemed a little childish. I don't even know where you went."

"You won't know where I went," Natalia replied. Fed up with her tone. "What makes you think you deserve to know?"

With anger rising back to the surface, Natalia took a few deep breaths, calming herself down before continuing.

"You walked out on me, remember? You threw away those seven years when you decided I wasn't even good enough to discuss your problems with." The burn of held-back tears had her despising Dan even more. "And quite frankly, you're an ignoramus if you think for one second that I have to explain, let alone answer at all to you anymore! If you don't understand why I didn't take you back, go and talk to Rick about it."

Slamming the phone shut, Natalia screamed and slammed her fist on the bed. How could she expect anything from her?

The audacity! Dan had some nerve!

She wasn't owed any explanation. If she needed one, she should go look in the mirror to find it.

I should never have let her get me that riled up, she chided herself.

Natalia pulled out some clothes from her bag and headed to the bathroom. Her inner voice yelling for her to forget Dan altogether and move on.

∽

"Well, I guess this is gonna have to do. I don't look too bad, just a little plain."

Grabbing a handful of hair, Nick frowned at her reflection while pulling it all into a ponytail. The light green button-down shirt stopped at her hips, coordinated with the white trousers that fell loosely over her white and green plaid heels.

After turning a few more times, she concluded this outfit would have to do. At least, that is what she told herself. Nick couldn't waste another half hour trying on clothes. Besides, she didn't want to be late.

Grabbing the listings, she found last night off the nightstand, she quickly scanned through them one last time. Sitting down in her lounge chair, she flipped open her phone and dialed Natalia's number. Her heart pounded with restrained anticipation, only to increase when the call was picked up on the fourth ring.

"Stop calling me! Leave me alone!"

Nick's heart paused at the flustered voice. The anger pierced her eardrums, causing her to flinch involuntarily.

Holding the phone a distance from her ear, she asked, "Ummm Natalia, is that you?"

Mentally, she braced herself for another round of yelling.

"This is Nick… Nick Ward," she rushed on, "I was wondering if you were still interested in going out today, but if you want me to leave you alone, I can."

Wow, she was irritated at something.

"I'm so sorry, it's just that… well, never mind." A slight pause and a shaky breath came across the line when Nick placed the receiver back against her ear.

"Yes, I still want to go out. It's still kind of early, isn't it? The last time I looked at the clock, it was eight am."

Shuffling could be heard in the background, and she assumed she was moving around.

"How soon did you want to go out?"

Noticing she sounded flustered, Nick had an overwhelming urge to comfort her and was a little put off by it.

Checking the clock on the wall, "It's nine am now. It is still a little early, though, if you want to grab some breakfast before we head out." Thinking the idea might help calm her down some. "Gracie makes a wonderful breakfast," Nick suggested.

"That sounds great."

A vision of a smile pulling Natalia's lips had Nick's heart skipping a beat.

"I haven't had breakfast yet."

The other woman's soft voice brought a calm to her, and she found the corner of her lips twitching in a smile.

"In fact, I didn't even get dinner last night, I was so tired I just fell into bed."

"I can be by around eleven to pick you up. Does that sound okay?"

The way her body was reacting to this woman had her on edge, and she wasn't sure if this was good or bad. Her heart thudded excitedly in her chest at the prospect of seeing her again.

"I'm finishing getting dressed now."

Nick opened her mouth to offer to eat with her but was cut off.

"I guess I'll see you around eleven then. Goodbye."

The abrupt end of the conversation left her disappointed. Unable to say goodbye. Nick had to wonder if Natalia was heterosexual and not interested in her at all.

I don't want to be presumptuous.

Whatever had Natalia acting like this, Nick only hoped that it wasn't her. Hopefully, by the time she got there to pick her up, Natalia would be in better spirits. Now it was time for her own breakfast and making last-minute phone calls before setting out for her day.

Without provoking, Nick's mind wandered back to images of her dream. Natalia, lying in bed, exhausted and naked from a night of passion, will forever be etched into her thoughts. The only thing that could erase that picture would be the real thing.

Chapter 6

Getting another long hot shower and throwing on comfy clothes helped relieve some of the tension Dan brought up. The day was too nice out to be feeling miserable and disheveled.

Natalia pushed her ex to the back of her mind while memories of her dream last night instantly made her blood pressure rise. Trying to be as comfortable as possible, Natalia settled on a dark green tank top with light tan shorts and white Nikes.

Descending down the staircase, one slow step at a time, calmed her nerves. Replaying the previous night's phone conversation had a sour feeling pitting in her stomach.

I should have never yelled at Nick. It was uncalled for.

Natalia could tell she had hurt her feelings. *Maybe I'll apologize again when I see her.*

The aroma of food wafted up to her from the dining room, rumbling her stomach. The smell brought her back to thirteen again at her grandmother's house.

Brushing her hair out of her face, she hurriedly went in search of the aroma. Locating her objective on a buffet counter, she grabbed a plate and filled it with a little bit of everything. Pouring herself a glass of iced tea on her way to the screened-in patio.

Searching the large area for a table with a view but not completely in the sun, Natalia settled on one in the far-left corner with a white lace tablecloth. Easing into a chair, preparing to eat, she saw Gracie strolling onto the patio.

Gracie's grey cotton button-down dress adorned with a big pink and white flower swayed as she waved jubilee. When Natalia waved back, Gracie made a beeline straight for her table. Her dress flowed around her as she walked. Taking the chair opposite of her, the other woman sat down with a plop. Her eye's seemed to glitter with her happy mood.

"So, how are you liking it so far? I didn't see you at dinner last night." She observed. "I figured you might have wanted to get some rest."

Natalia offered to get her some food or a drink but Gracie declined with a shake of her head.

"I fell right to sleep last night." She explained, taking a bite. "I didn't even realize I was that tired."

Attempting to keep the food in her mouth, she tried not to open too much while she ate.

"The room is just fine, and you were right. That view is amazing!"

Natalia swallowed and took another bite, "I hope I find something with a view like that today." Pausing, she sipped her tea before gorging herself some more.

"I'm just glad you're enjoying your stay." The other woman paused till Natalia met her eyes.

"So, you're going out today? Who's taking you? I mean… if you don't mind me asking."

Seeming not to mind that Natalia was filling her face with food, Gracie relaxed back into her chair and smiled at her.

Natalia returned her smile, feeling a fondness for the older woman.

"I don't mind at all. I'm officially starting my first day of house hunting today.

Finishing off her plate, she pushed it aside.

"I'm going out with Nick Ward. I just hope I don't get too flustered looking." Giving voice to her concerns. "Some people go nuts just trying to decide on the right cosmetic fixes that they completely break down when it comes to the actual bidding part."

Natalia picked up her cup, easing back into her chair. Sipping lazily while Gracie spoke.

"Well, I don't fully understand the whole process anyway." Dismissing with a wave of her hand, "But Nick is a good girl. Very strong-willed and bright. She'll be able to steer you right."

Stopping, Gracie looked around the room, "Oh, and speak of the girl, here she comes."

Rising from her seat, Gracie pulled Nick into a warm embrace. Natalia sat up straight and placed her cup down. A flush crept up her neck at the sight of Nick. The mere presence of this woman made chills run up her spine. The flush traveled up her cheeks as Nick's eye landed on hers.

Eyes darting between the two women, Gracie's mouth tilted up in a knowing smirk. Quickly getting the hint, she excused herself.

"Well, I'll leave you two to your business. Don't have her back too late, missy," Waving a finger at Nick, "I want her to at least have a good night's dinner tonight."

Taking notice Gracie wouldn't leave until she agreed, Nick confirmed she would have her back at a reasonable time. Natalia felt they were being treated like teenagers. Nodding and narrowing her eyes, Gracie went to the other tables to mingle with the guests.

Giggling, Natalia noticed Nick's gaze travel up and down her body briefly as she stood. Their eyes locked, and the giggle died in her throat.

Confused, *was Nick checking me out?*

Her frown was replaced with a smile when she saw the approving grin wash over Nick's face. Her insides warmed, and she cleared her throat. Nick's focus came back to her and why she was there.

"So, are we setting off now, or did you want to stick around here a while longer?" She nodded at the table. "I'm ready to go whenever you are." Nick's voice was flat and serious. A complete contrast to the glitter of humor in her eyes.

Now, it was Nick's turn to blush, having been caught unabashedly staring at Natalia. Nick couldn't seem to help herself. Natalia couldn't complain either, having been caught doing the same thing yesterday.

She is like eye candy.

From the expression on Natalia's face, it didn't seem as though the other woman minded in the least.

"Nice outfit." Natalia watched Nick lick her bottom lip. Not acknowledging the compliment with a reply.

It scared her slightly to know that she wasn't the only one feeling this attraction - or whatever it was - between them. Natalia needed to keep this as professional as possible, and to do that, she would have to keep her distance.

"I'm ready right now. I'll let you clean up, and I'll meet you outside."

With a creak of the chair legs, Nick rose and quickly turned around. Natalia didn't know if she hurt her feelings or if she embarrassed her, but she watched as Nick fled the dining room.

Ok...

Chapter 7

"Wow, that house was outrageously too big for me. How many square feet was it?"

Natalia didn't wait for Nick to respond.

"It doesn't matter. I don't think I need something that big. I liked the lot size, but the house… it was too choppy, and what was with that barn?"

Nick watched her rub at her temple and wished she could make this process easier for her.

"It looked like they renovated part of the house and just left the barn to fall to pieces. *Literately.*"

Natalia threw her hands up in exasperation at Nick's light-hearted chuckle.

"They expect people to pay all that money to still have to fix more problems? Something isn't right with that."

Nick cut the engine after turning into the parking lot of the deli where they had lunch yesterday.

"You're mostly paying for the lot size and the equity that went into the remodel of the house." She explained as best as she could.

Understanding the frustration that comes with house hunting, her professional tone rang out. At the look Natalia gave her, she figured giving her personal opinion wouldn't hurt.

"I do see your point. It does seem to be a bit overpriced and that barn was scary looking."

Scrunching her nose, Nick stuck her tongue out to lighten the mood. Even though Natalia rolled her eyes, she was successful in her endeavor.

"We looked at more houses than just that one, though. You didn't look like you clicked really with any of them. You're not getting discouraged yet, are you?"

Looking directly into her eyes, Nick tried to figure out precisely what she was thinking. Guessing how she peered at her and licked her lips, she knew it was a mistake. Staring into those beautiful green eyes, her body warmed. Tingles radiated from her toes and traveled to her chest.

She had been caught staring numerous times as they walked the properties. Keeping her eyes off the other woman was harder said than done. Everything about her- from her Nike-clad feet to her beautiful hair, had Nick's body humming.

On more than one occasion, she could have sworn she had seen a desire ripple across Natalia's eyes before, but like a flash of lightning, it was gone.

Kind of like now.

The first time Nick brushed it off as her mind playing tricks on her, but when it happened again, she couldn't deny Natalia must have feelings for her too. Sure, Nick went back and forth a few times.

A woman as gorgeous and accomplished as her would be straight, right?

But then Nick would see her staring, and she would wonder.

She's a client, for God's sake. I need to keep my distance before I can't control myself. Besides she probably isn't all that interested in me anyway.

Pushing down her intruding thoughts, Nick smiled. The beautiful woman in front of her also shaking her head.

"Not at all. I just really haven't found the feeling I'm looking for, I guess."

Taking a few moments to retrieve herself, Nick replayed the conversation they were having. Getting herself back on track.

"I guess I just thought it would be going more smoothly than what it is. The actual house hunting hasn't been going very well," Natalia scrunched her nose and smiled at Nick. "The company sure has been the highlight of my day so far."

Without another word, Natalia opened her door and stepped out of the car. Nick sat there, trying to decide if what she had just heard was a come-on or if she was just being friendly.

No, she is just complimenting her realtor.

Dismissing the notion with a shake of her head, she joined Natalia in the warm mid-summer sun.

During lunch, they went over the pros and cons of the properties they already saw. Nick jotted down notes and compiled a list of more suitable homes to view on her lap. Every so often Nick would pause to sip some of her tea and see Natalia watching her, creating a stir low in her belly.

Ignoring the invading thoughts, she focused on Natalia's list. The updated features were nice but she preferred the older homes for their antique charm. Chatting while they ate, Nick had to catch herself several times during their conversation as her mind would continue to wander away with unbidden thoughts.

Caressing Natalia's back while kissing her neck or rubbing her thumb over swollen lips after feasting on them. Wondering if her neck felt as soft as it looked, and once, she almost reached out to touch it.

When Natalia would laugh, Nick could smell her perfume floating all around them. A mix of lilac and cherry blossoms teased her senses, sending her pulse racing. Lifting her hand to her head twice to check if she had a fever, only for Natalia to question if she was all right. Shrugging it off as "too much sun," Nick left it at that.

It became mentally draining, having to calm herself down time and again. Surprisingly, Nick was able to discuss the next couple of houses she had planned to show her this evening.

One was an older farmhouse on 2 acres. The owners couldn't afford to keep it anymore and needed to move out of state. Next, she had an updated colonial with many extras to offer that she thought Natalia would like but it has a smaller size lot. Lastly, she wanted to take her by a rancher that had an addition added onto it, including a screened-in porch with a new barn out back. The barn comes with an already fenced-in pasture too.

Natalia loomed over the photos of the properties, a piece of hair falling to the front of her face. The long brown strand teased as it glittered in the summer sun, tempting Nick to reach out and brush it back.

After what seemed like an hour but was closer to twenty, she couldn't stand it anymore. Nick reached out, gently pushing the strand behind the other woman's ear.

Her eyes shot to Natalia's when a hand grabbed her wrist. Her desire mirrored back at her. Secretly, Nick had been sinking deeper and deeper since picking her up this morning.

Nothing moved; time stood still. The air was thick with unsaid promises as neither of them breathed. Those eyes got darker as seconds passed.

The silence was broken by the loud chirp of a phone ringing. Both women jumped at the intruding noise. Natalia blinked rapidly, then turned around to pull a phone from her pocket. Instantly, Nick felt the loss of connection, making her feel cold inside. Natalia was distracted by the phone screen, she missed the slight shiver Nick released.

Sighing, she let it go to voice mail. "I'm sorry. It's been so long since..."

Trailing off and dropping her gaze to the table, she continued, "I got caught up in the moment. If I made you uncomfortable, you can just drop me back off at the B & B."

Confused over the frown across the other woman's face, Nick had an awkward moment of opening and closing her mouth. She didn't want the sudden change in mood to be because of her.

"No, it's okay." She assured her. "We can still go looking."

Nick rushed on. Her words tumbled out of her mouth like a hurricane. "I know what you mean. I haven't been intimate with anyone in years." She blurted out. "The last girlfriend I had was back in my college days. So, I can understand what you're feeling."

At Natalia's wide eyes, Nick felt more heat flush her already warm cheeks.

Great, just dig a bigger hole, Nick... women love the over-sharing.

Her words had them both blushing. Nick couldn't believe she divulged that tidbit of information.

I can't believe I assumed Natalia was thinking...

Clasping her hands together on the table kept Nick from reaching out. Clearing her throat once again, she continued, "If you're ready, we can go ahead and look at the other properties. I do have to get you back kind of early tonight."

Natalia's brows furrowed.

"I promised Gracie I'd have you back in time for dinner." She explained with a chuckle. "Feels like I'm back in school." Blushing and rolling her eyes in amusement.

Relaxing her shoulders, Natalia smiled showing off her beautiful features. The energy around them softening as the stress melted away, graciously replaced by quiet contentment.

"I'm glad it isn't school all over again. I didn't enjoy it very much the first time around." Natalia emphasized with a show of sticking out her tongue.

Oh, how I would love to suck that into my mouth, the little voice in Nick's head taunted.

Composing herself, Nick straightened and rolled her shoulders back.

"I guess we really should get going then, if we are going to see all the houses you have lined up for tonight."

Rising at that, Nick took their trays and emptied them into the trash can. Nodding, Natalia took one more sip of her drink before dumping the rest into the trash. Grateful for the chance, Nick held open the cafe door and watched Natalia's movements as she walked past. The ability to take in her curves without judgment, she sighed and followed close behind.

With the heat hitting her like a wall, Nick took a few deep breaths. The weather was not kind in some aspects. The corner of Natalia's mouth tipped up as Nick held the passenger door open for her. A warm sensation rushed over her body, and Nick found herself mimicking that same half-smile.

Once seated, Nick closed the door and hurried around to get herself situated in the driver's seat. Now both settled in the car, and the air conditioner turned on high, Nick pulled out, and they drove off together in peaceful silence.

෴

"So, you finally call me, and when you do it's only to talk about some hot realtor that you met?!"

From the sound of Rachel's voice, Natalia knew her friend was smiling and teasing her.

"Sounds like you're already enjoying yourself."

She threw her hands up in the air in surrender, forgetting she couldn't be seen through the phone. Her hands plopped back down to her sides.

"When do I get to come and visit? Did you find a house yet?"

"No," Exhaustion mingled with irritation for a second before she caught herself. "I haven't found a house that I like yet."

Sighing loudly in the empty room, "You know you can come whenever you'd like to. That is, if you can get time off."

Natalia sat on the bed and pulled her shoes off. Rubbing the pads of her feet gave her so much pleasure that she moaned lightly.

"How are you liking the clinic without me?"

Another moan escaped her lips.

"Dr. Riggin's treating you well?"

"Well -"

Moving from rubbing her feet to her neck, she didn't catch Rachel replying.

"I am hurt that you think the only reason I called you was to gloat about my realtor! Besides… who said she was hot? I don't recall saying anything like that."

Not that I can deny it.

"All I said was she wasn't bad-looking and was nice."

Now it was Rachel's turn to be thrown off by an assault of questions. Natalia chastised herself earlier when she realized she had yet to check in with Rachel. However, when she got in, Gracie, in her button-up yellow sundress, gave no time to decline, pulling Nick and her into the dining room.

The sun had started to set, and neither of them recalled how late it was as they were rushed to a table and had food plopped down in front of them. Both women mentioned that something felt off about the situation, but instead of analyzing it, they simply enjoyed each other's company.

Three hours had gone by in a flash. Fascinated by how easy it is to talk to such a beautiful woman. Not once did she itch to run from feeling like she was a bug on a shoe. The more she found out about Nick, the more intrigued she became. The line between professional and intimate starting to get dangerously thin.

By the time they finished their food, Natalia was yawning into her arm. Nick, once again, had gotten up and removed their plates, which she was grateful for. The disappointing 'goodnight' led to an endearing hug. For a moment, she lost all common sense and kissed her cheek.

Uh, oh.

The air was sucked out of the room, and they were the only two left on the earth. Soft candlelight flickered within the dining room while everything else faded away. Unconsciously, Natalia pulled Nick's body flush with hers and smelled her hair. The scent of roses mingled with their embrace, the feeling so natural.

Nonetheless, reality rushed back. Natalia's brain turned back on, and she broke away from the warmth. The loss of contact not lost on either of them. With a nod, Nick walked away. Natalia sighed, slumped her shoulders, and made her way to her room, feeling light-headed and exhausted.

Maybe the move and house hunting are getting to me.

"Nat! Hey, you there?!"

Natalia shook her head and blinked a few times. The phone almost slipped from her hand as she remembered she was still holding it.

She replied in a confused voice, "Yes."

"Wow, you like… really went into a zone."

A chortling laugh filled her ear.

"Anyway, like I was saying, *lesbian*, the new Doc is nice, but he doesn't get along with the clients as well as you did."

Pausing, she heard rustling, and Rachel's voice was hushed when she started up again. "Mrs. Nunez stopped coming here. She didn't want a male Veterinarian. I feel bad for her."

Mrs. Nunez was an elderly lady who donated a lot of money to the clinic. That wasn't good news for her old practice.

"On another note," her voice returned to normal, "I should be able to get away for a few days next week. I can't wait!"

Natalia pulled the receiver away from her ear at the squeal that erupted.

"I definitely need a vacation." A snort and a giggle, "By the way, you didn't have to say your realtor was hot; I could tell just by the way you were talking."

A low whistle came in from the other end.

"You were talking more about her than the houses that you didn't like."

Imagining her friend wiggling her eyebrows made Natalia chuckle to herself.

"Besides, both you and I know that you're not going to do anything about this."

Natalia rolled her eyes at that statement.

"So, when I get down there, I expect to meet this woman who has stolen your conscience and given you ADD."

The laugh that bubbled up her throat broke into the quiet room with a rumble. Her ears vibrated with the sound, reverberating down her body. For some reason, Rachel always knew how to make her smile, even when she didn't want to. Laughter died down while she panted for a few moments, trying to catch her breath.

On the other end, Rachel was still in a fit of giggles. Rachel only stopped to end the call before rushing to hang up. Natalia agreed to remember to call her again tomorrow night, as the line went dead.

Finally, alone with her thoughts, she replayed the events of the day like snapshots in her mind. Nick's company is a welcome change. Their chemistry as natural as eating.

You know better, Natalia. She is your employee.

Never mixing business with her personal life had a bit of anxiety creeping in, and she wasn't even sure the woman felt the same. Still, there was an attraction she couldn't deny. Drawn to her like a moth to a light, her mind wandered to the gorgeous strawberry blonde - who, just hours earlier - captured her attention.

Throwing on pajamas, Natalia laid across her sheets. Her body hummed. Warmth radiated from her skin, and she wasn't sure if the summer heat or her naughty thoughts causing this reaction.

Either way, she pushed the covers lower in an attempt to cool herself. Images of beautifully intense dark green eyes staring at her filled the back of her eyelids, helping her to sleep.

Chapter 8

Stretching against the heat of the steadily rising sun, her bones cracked, and she wiped at the sleepiness still clinging to her eyelids. Blinking them open, the ceiling came into view. Natalia had enormous amounts of energy after finally catching her first full night's sleep in months.

Without her normal morning headache, she hopped herself out of bed, looking forward to the challenge of home searching. Not letting the events of yesterday detour her from finding a home, she grabbed her clothes to get a long, relaxing hot shower, washing away any lingering feelings of defeat from yesterday. A half-hour later, showered and dressed, Natalia checked her phone on her way downstairs for breakfast.

She found Nick already sitting at a table talking to Gracie. Surprise mingled with excitement at seeing her. Natalia stood back in the doorway, surveying her. Drinking in all of the lush curves and sensuous movements of her body. The muscles in her neck stretched against her blue polo shirt when she laughed at whatever Gracie was saying to her.

Standing there staring, felt like she was doing something naughty, like stalking or voyeurism. Observing, while Nick was completely oblivious to it, made Natalia aroused. An energized sensation filed her body, but she couldn't look away.

A part of her wondered at her inability to see where this might lead.

I wonder…

Still, she wasn't sure if the other woman was interested or not. Not everyone was a lesbian, she had found that out that hard way when she was younger. So, why is she trying so hard to keep her distance?

Maybe because you're still trying to regain your life after Dan ripped it to shreds? Or, how about that she's your employee, per se, by being your realtor?

The voice in her head nagged at her. Her subconscious told her to back off, but her insides screamed a different tune. The hum between her thighs grew painful, and the pounding of her heart all but thrummed out of her chest when their eyes locked. How Nick looked back at her, had her needing to be touched. Her body aching for it.

∽

This day felt almost perfect from the moment she woke up. The sun shimmers off every surface through the open window. The light breeze hit her skin, cooling her from the sweltering heat of the morning. Starting the morning with a warm bath and the guarantee of seeing a beautiful woman was all she could ever ask for in life.

Stepping through the oak door to the B&B, Gracie ushered her to a table, already set with a plate full of food. The typical comforting hospitality and conversation as she ate her eggs and bacon made her feel even more blessed. Gracie was a great friend.

Always there to lend an ear or fill your tummy. Knowing many people in and around town, Nick had very few close friends. From the moment she met Gracie, the elderly lady had become family.

Hearing that she was here alone, she would make sure she always had a meal. Using it as an excuse to poke and prod until Nick spilled her guts about her past. Now, all these years later, they are accustomed to their daily rituals.

Laughing as Gracie went on about finding ferrets in the laundry brought memories of other things that have happened at the B & B over the years. Catching her breath, Gracie waved her arm around.

"Just when I was about to call animal control, Frankie, the son of the lady staying in suite 4, came bounding down the stairs in search of them."

Her face lit up in amusement at the recollection.

"He didn't want his mom to know that he couldn't leave home without them!" Unable to control herself, Gracie broke out in laughter again.

But Nick wasn't laughing. Instead, she had her sight locked on the woman across the room. Natalia was breathtaking in her lilac dress. The neckline plummeted into a V, stopping just before it hit the top of her breast. The length showed off her irresistible tan legs, with light purple flip-flops.

A feral need filled her, making her mouth go dry as she admired her like a painting. With her hair pulled back into a braid, Nick's eyes followed the curve of Natalia's neck in a visual caress.

It looked so soft that her fingers itched to reach out and run over the tender flesh. Instead, she clasped her hands together under the table and clenched her teeth.

Natalia's eyes met hers, and she realized she had been caught. The other woman visibly shivered. The slight movement caused Nick to shift in her seat. The room became increasingly warm.

What I wouldn't give to run my hands over the skin of her neck.

Nick shook her head.

I don't understand myself lately. One minute, I am the model of control; the next, I want to throw reason out the window and take her in my arms.

Through her racing heart and shallow breaths, Nick realized something was missing from her perfect morning. It was Natalia. She had never experienced a lightbulb effect before. Nick's chest became tight and it felt like the wind had been knocked out of her.

"Darling, are you okay?" Gracie frowned. Worry lines showing on her forehead. "You're looking a little flushed."

The other woman's voice was a gentle hum against the rushing in her ears.

"Are you listening to me?" She questioned. Nick's focused turn towards Gracie. Her brows furrowed together in concern.

"I'll be fine."

Gracie raised one eyebrow.

"I will be. I promise." She tried to assure her. "I think my thoughts just ran away with me again."

Gracie raised her other eyebrow and smiled warmly, turning her eyes in the direction Nick's had been seconds ago. Nick averted her gaze before Gracie could give her that knowing look she was anticipating.

"Ah, ok." Gracie slid her chair back. "I have to get going anyway. Too many things to check up on, but I will stop back by later."

Sighing internally at the relief washing over her, Nick stood and wrapped the other woman in a hug before watching her saunter off to another table.

She pushed her chair in and made her way toward Natalia. Ignoring the flip flops growing in her stomach with every step.

"You look great." Nick complimented. "I take it you got enough rest?"

Nick had to keep herself from reaching out when Natalia brushed a loose strand of her hair. Mentally chiding herself to get a handle over her reactions. It was hard with the beautiful creature standing in front of her.

"Ready to go, or did you want to grab some breakfast?"

Natalia was already shaking her head before the end of her question.

"I'm not hungry anymore. I will probably be by the time we go for lunch."

Natalia smiled brightly and shifted her body to angle towards the doorway.

Was she nervous too?

"You look rested."

"I feel great this morning. Thank you for noticing." She beamed another smile. "I passed out when my head hit the pillow. It was the best sleep I have had in a long time."

The small awkward chuckle sent a shiver up her spine. "Let's get going, shall we?"

Natalia turned, sweeping her arm out, waiting for Nick to walk past her. For a brief moment, their eyes locked.

I could melt into those eyes.

Shaking her head helped to clear her mind. She had a feeling she would be doing that a lot around her.

"I can have lunch, but it will have to be an early one. I have another couple that I am showing a home to later on." Nick smiled and proceeded to walk past Natalia, adding, "So let's get going."

Chapter 9

Staying at the B&B, while a wonderful experience, was starting to feel like her life was at a standstill when all she wanted to do was move forward. A whole week of browsing, viewing, and scanning through homes was exhausting. Looking at the computer screen or her phone became a nuisance.

The never-ending cycle strained her nerves horribly, that Natalia was reluctant to go out and search anymore. Hating looking at house after house without even the echo in her mind of wanting to make an offer, was taking its toll. How people could go through this for months or even years, Natalia couldn't even fathom.

Today was going to be a relaxing and exciting day, she thought to herself.

Her best friend was coming for a three-day visit. From the moment Rachel mentioned it, her body became a jittery mess, leaving her to toss and turn most of the night.

Catching up should be fun.

Cupping her mouth, she let out another yawn. Rachel sounded worn down when they spoke on the phone. Her friend needed this break. She had been having trouble adjusting to the new veterinarian and didn't know what to do about it.

Concerned about her stress level, Natalia mentioned taking time off. Rachel was contemplating taking early retirement, but she wasn't truly ready to give up working just yet. Without having anyone to come home to, Rachel mostly spent her time with the 'little people' who needed her. Natalia always smiled at the nickname she gave to the animals at the clinic.

Wishing she had a house picked out to show her, she grimaced at the length of time it had taken even to make a decision. Last night, she informed Nick that any of the houses she was scheduled to see this week would have to be canceled. Against pausing the house hunt, Nick had argued that it would be best not to let them all simply slip by.

"Anyone can put an offer in at any time and snatch your dream home," she had quipped into the receiver.

With her mind already made up - knowing she needed a break from the endless disappointments, Natalia resolutely agreed only to cancel for two days but informed Nick that her friend would be joining them after that. No way was she leaving her friend behind in her room to look at properties.

Completely in control the entire time, Nick changed their schedule around without complaining or missing a beat. It was sexy to hear a confident woman take charge sometimes. Towards the end of their call, Nick was a bit sullener sounding. Her tone softened, and she paused briefly before asking about the weather.

A nervous chatter filled her head, and she bit her lip. Opening her mouth to ask if she was okay, Nick abruptly said she needed to go and hung up the phone. Stunned at the sudden click, Natalia pulled her phone away from her ear and stared at it for a few seconds.

The echo of the click rang in her ear, leaving an odd sensation in her stomach.

What in the world was that all about? Should I call her back?

Her phone felt heavy in her hand. Her hair fluttered around her as she shook her head, deciding it was best to leave it alone. Natalia finished getting ready for her guests' arrival. Excitement and a pinch of anxiety flowed through her as she bounded down the stairs like a ten-year-old going on an Easter egg hunt. Nothing but smiles and anticipation painted her face.

"Slow down, their young lady."

Almost bumping into Gracie when she slipped in the foyer. Tiny wrinkles pulled in the corner of her eyes, giving an aura of wisdom.

"Where's the fire? Or do you have a hot date I didn't hear about?"

The teasing tone didn't hide the underlying prodding of information. Clasping her hands in front of her, Natalia lightly swayed on her heels. The conversation comforting and warmed her heart to know that even if she was on her own out here, at least someone cared enough to ask her about her day.

"Well, if you must know, I have company coming this morning."

Barely able to contain her excitement, she bit back a squeal.

"My friend is visiting from Tennessee, and I can't wait to show her around. It feels like months since I've seen her, which is just silly because it's only been about two weeks."

Full of energy, Gracie's watchful gaze scanned Natalia as she shifted from foot to foot.

"It'll feel like that often when you're hanging around this town." Nodding her head, "Maybe if you got out more and met some new people, you wouldn't feel so lonely. And I mean to do more than look at houses", she added with a smirk.

"Although, it will be nice to see some new faces around here."

Tapping a finger on her chin with a look of contemplation, Natalia stood up straighter.

"You should bring her to dinner after you kids finish up running around." She went on to say, "I'd sure like to meet her, and I could make my post-roast." Her hand fell to her lap, and a tender smile played on her lips.

A hand lifted and patted her on the shoulder. Gracie made her way around Natalia and began cleaning up breakfast. Watching the woman as she wiped down tables and swayed around chairs. Natalia smiled when she began to lightly hum to herself.

At the sound of a car pulling up out front, her head whipped around. A door opening and slamming shut brought her attention back to her day's plans. Moving her legs, which now felt like jelly, she made her way outside to greet her friend.

Chapter 10

"Now that I'm finally here, you have nothing planned!? I am not just sitting around to watch the world go by. By lunch, I will have gone insane."

The taunting etches to her voice would fool anyone else into believing Rachel was a bit perturbed, but Natalia knew better.

Sighing, she dropped her bag at the foot of the bed. Stress chiseled all over Rachel's features, making Natalia ache inside.

"Oh, and by the way, everyone at the clinic said to tell you 'Hi.' They all miss you, and some of them keep asking me if you've started a new clinic so they can follow you."

The light chuckle contrasted the look of disdain and weariness in her eyes. A sour feeling rested at the pit of her stomach, making her feel a bit sick.

"I thought they were joking at first, but after being asked a couple of days in a row…., I almost had to hold a meeting to remind them all that you went on retirement." Natalia giggled at her friend when she made a show of sighing and rolling her eyes. "I don't need any more rumors running around."

"We don't want that now, do we?"

Natalia added. Her words dripped with mock annoyance and humor.

"Besides, half of them probably wouldn't be able to handle all the green and wet humidity out here." She paused, checking the time. "So, you want to get out around town? I don't know too many places since all I have been out looking at is houses, but I guess we could both go exploring if you want to."

The smile that flew across Rachel's face made her almost regret moving. Even with lines of stress around her eyes still, Rachel always radiated beauty, but when she was happy and excited, it permeated everything around her with beauty too.

She used to wonder why she wasn't in love with Rachel. After a while, their friendship blossomed and Rachel had become family. Once, they discussed it when Rachel got drunk. Both of them concluded that their friendship meant too much to ruin and never discussed it again.

Quickly, she scanned the balcony area behind Rachel. "That sounds great! We could just take a relaxing day of driving. Maybe well find some interesting spots."

Turning around, Rachel gave an interrogating stare. The hair on Natalia's neck perked up. She could only guess what Rachel was thinking.

"So… you've been out an awful lot with this realtor woman." Glittering eyes and a tilt to one corner of her mouth had her rolling her eyes. "Do I ever get to meet her? Have you asked her out yet?"

Yup, not getting out of this line of questioning.

"I've already told you I'm keeping it professional. You'll get to meet her in a few days when we go house hunting again." Expelling air from her lungs, made her lightheaded for a second. "I know you'll be dying to do that." The sarcasm in her voice was not lost on Rachel.

Ignoring the last half of what Natalia said, Rachel went on with her prodding of questions. "I still don't see what the problem is. You can keep it professional and still get a little action." The tone more serious now. "You know you like her, so I don't understand why you don't want to give it a chance. It doesn't have anything to do with Dan, does it?"

Rachel mimicked her when she narrowed her eyes. "Like I've already said, it is remaining professional."

She responded with finality. Rachel didn't press any further. Instead, she excused herself to the bathroom. Natalia, grateful for the small reprieve, collected her thoughts before Rachel emerged. Neither one of them picked up the conversation again. Bounding down the stairs, Natalia was excited to begin their day of exploration.

$\mathcal{C}$hapter 11

Today was exactly what they both needed. Going with the flow had them stumbling upon various antique shops, a market, a garage, three restaurants, a police department, a fire station, and what seemed to resemble a small church. Grabbing a quick lunch at the deli Natalia had grown accustomed to in the short amount of time she had been there was perfect.

Under the watchful gaze of the morning sun, they made small talk. Discussing the latest updates in a new vaccine that should be available within the next month. A light wind blew around them, cooling her skin for brief seconds before the sun beat down on her once again. Finishing up lunch, they decided to visit the SPCA they passed at the edge of town.

Walking in through the front doors, Natalia was greeted by the familiar smells of animals and ammonia. From the outside, the shelter looked tiny, with its boxed brick edges and low-hanging porch, but when she walked in, she was pleasantly surprised by the open feeling of the foyer. It was massive.

"Nice setup," Rachel murmured what Natalia was thinking.

A gift shop lined with banners to the right of them had several signs that caught her eye. They pointed towards the back, directing people to a kitten and puppy section, a cat and dog section, a reptile section, and lastly, a wild rescue section.

Natalia saw another sign at the front desk for the stable outside that explained they housed cows, horses, goats, pigs, sheep, geese, ducks, cocks, hens, lamas, and alpacas. The list was very impressive.

She almost felt a little dizzy looking back and forth through all the hallways of plexiglass. They made their way to the round welcome desk directly in front of the entrance.

Natalia noticed a generously tall young man behind it. Rolling his brown eyes, he mumbled under his breath as he hung up the phone. Plastering on a smile, he placed his hands on the counter and cheerfully greeted both women.

In her usual doctor persona, Natalia skipped the small talk. "Good morning." She said, squaring her shoulder and smiling back. "I'm new in town. My friend and I noticed your shelter and thought we'd drop in to check it out."

The young man pushed off the counter and squared his shoulders. His thick eyebrows raised slightly. He opened his mouth to speak but closed it again when Natalia continued her conversation.

"I also didn't notice any Veterinary clinics on my way here. Do you happen to know where I might find one?"

Glancing over her shoulder, she noticed Rachel wandering over to the donation desk next to the gift shop. Amused at her inability to stand still.

His smile faltered slightly, and he shook his head. "As for a Veterinary clinic, you're standing in it."

A noise from the computer on the desk distracted him; he leaned over and pushed a key on the keypad before turning his attention back to her.

"We're not only the SPCA, but we also provide the only Veterinary care in town."

His words had her frowning, and her brows drew together in confusion. The next words out of his mouth didn't make her feel much better either.

"The closest clinic to us is about 50 miles north in Crest Fall. Our shelter has two veterinarians and five technicians who work here. Other than that, we mostly operate on volunteers. The number of staff on-site ranges from day to day, but we average roughly fifteen a day."

The young man leans and pulls out a pamphlet from a stack on the counter and hands it to her. Pointing to it, he proudly states, "We have a no-kill policy, so the more help, the better. If you'd like, I could set you up with an appointment for one of the vets."

Turning towards the computer again, she noticed him mumble something to himself. In one swift motion, he gripped the mouse and gave it a few clicks, looking back and forth from the screen to her. Natalia looked down at the pamphlet.

"That's ok."

"Or you could go down the hall to their office. It's the fourth door on the right."

Sitting down, he pointed down the hallway to the left. A big grin returned to his face, causing her to smile in return. Guessing he gets asked similar questions a lot because not once during their conversation did he pause. His speech came out seamless, and she figured he had practiced repeating it. Natalia couldn't help but be impressed.

She shifted her feet as she looked down at the pamphlet in her hands. Briefly scanning the inside, noting certain bits of information before closing it and looking back up at the man.

"I wouldn't mind meeting the Vet, but perhaps another time." Sighing, she crossed her arms. "It is surprising you only have two veterinarians for this whole county. Don't you get a little backed up?"

"Sometimes, but when you're in such a small town, they are hard to find. We are just glad to have the help we do have."

The phone rings again, and they both turn to stare at it.

"Now, if you'll excuse me," he nods at the phone. "I have to get back."

Picking up the phone, he greets the caller while still looking at her. Whoever is on the other end, he politely asks them to please hold and covers the end of the receiver.

"If you have any other questions, one of the volunteers will be able to assist you. Thank you for visiting." He finishes with a nod.

Natalia softly thanked him for his time as he removed his hand and lifted the receiver to his ear. Shrugging, she returns her attention back to finding Rachel. Wondering through the halls didn't prove to be very fruitful. To help her in her quest, she asked a few of the animals if they had seen her, but their communication skills were lacking. Without any progress, she decided to go to the one place she knew Rachel would wander.

Walking up to the Veterinary clinic's door, she noted the sign on the door that said Last Hope Veterinary Clinic, with a Dr. Withers name plate underneath. Her body lightly shook, holding in a laugh at the irony of the name of the clinic corresponding with the last name of the Veterinarian.

Composing herself with a few deep breaths, a notable heavy scent of citrus wafted up her nose. Whoever cleaned the clinic must have used a lot of cleaning spray.

They clearly had a craving for the smell of citrus.

Pulling on the door, the scent became increasingly intense. Natalia held back a cough as her nose flared. Breathing through her nose to adjust to the odor. Green cushions lined long benches against three walls. Matching chairs in the middle surrounded a wooden table to complete the decent-sized waiting room.

Cream-colored walls highlighted the light spilling into the space from the expanse of windows lining the left side of the room. The generous view out onto the pond softened the clinical feeling of the room and made it more inviting.

A jovial voice infused the air and she scanned the room, finding Rachel at the far-right side of the reception counter flirting with the receptionist. Walking through an otherwise quiet but fully occupied waiting room, familiar feelings came to her. The familiar sounds and atmosphere reminding her of her clinic in Tennessee brought a calm contentment over her as she approached the counter.

Rachel never could get away from any semblance of work. It was in her blood, which is probably what drew her attention to the office, but that's not what was holding her attention now. Flirting with the woman behind the glass, Rachel was unaware of Natalia standing beside her.

"The girls back home remind me of a tornado. They carry you off, then drop you when they're done with you."

The receptionist broke out in a light laugh while Rachel stood there, a smug look on her face. Proud of the reaction she got, Rachel leaned heavily on the counter. The smitten look the receptionist was displaying had Natalia inwardly groaning.

"Are you stealing lines from me again?"

Rachel jumped and let out a noise that resembled a squawk, making the receptionist snort with laughter. A flinch of tension before Rachel turned around. Redness crept up her neck, flushing her cheeks.

"Don't do that. You scared that crap outta me."

Wide-eyed, she turned back to the receptionist.

"Evelyn, this is my good friend Dr. Natalia Purez."

Rachel stepped aside as the two women shook hands.

"So, what kind of Doctor are you?"

Before Natalia could answer, Rachel spoke.

"She's a veterinarian. The best back in Tennessee."

Natalia bit back a protest at the praise.

"But she decided to take an early retirement and settle down."

The half sarcastic solemn tone didn't fool her. Her friend understood how much this move meant to her, and she saw her smiling with every word.

"Really?!" Evelyn's face lit up. The pitch of her voice rose. "You know we're in need of a Vet here if you get bored with retirement…"

Evelyn winked at Rachel. Without missing a beat, she started talking about the benefits of working at the clinic. How it was a great place to meet people and a wonderful working environment. Mentally agreeing that she missed the emotional gratification of working in a clinic, Natalia reminded herself why she moved in the first place.

"You sure you really want to retire?" Rachel chimed in. Both of them trying to entice her into reentering the workforce.

Natalia sighs and shakes her head. The corner of her mouth tipping up when Evelyn sits up straighter in her chair and begins again.

"We could use the help. There is a lack of veterinarians around here."

Natalia raises a hand. "I'll think about it." She said, smirking and dropping her hand to her side. Evelyn frowned and Rachel stuck out her bottom lip in a sarcastic pout. Rolling her eyes, Natalia pulls out her business card and hands it to Evelyn.

Voice dripping with disappointment, Evelyn concedes for the time being.

"Thanks. I'll give it to Dr. Withers."

Natalia patted Rachel on the shoulder, signifying that she was ready to go. Nodding, she slid Evelyn a piece of paper with her phone number and asked her out for a drink. Leaning over on the counter, Evelyn agreed with a wink. Walking away, Natalia knew her friend was mentally making plans for the next time she would be visiting.

Maybe she will be moving too, she grinned to herself.

$\mathcal{C}$*hapter* 12

I can't believe how many there are. Why do people do this? It's horrible.

Sounds of sorrowful whines filled the room. Howls and mews of frustrated animals needing attention pulled at her consciousness.

I really could see myself taking so many of them home, but can I really do this?

Nick came into the shelter on a whim. Her last clients, a couple in their early twenties, were entirely touchy-feely. The way they made doe eyes and kissy faces at each other had her craving companionship. Tired of always coming home to nothing but empty silence, she decided to give adoption a try.

Making her way around several cages, she came across a grey floppy-eared rabbit named Tipsy and a grey and white long-haired cat named Smokey. Their soft fur and calm demeanor pulled her attention. Although, she was starting to have doubts.

What in the world would I do with a rabbit? Visions of a cage that would just sit till she had time to clean it filled her mind. *At least a cat can take care of itself most of the time.*

It's always been just her. Without having something else to demand her attention, she became used to the low-maintenance lifestyle. A fluttering heart had her pausing when she started dwelling on being responsible for someone else's life. Her head spun, and sadness crept up her throat as she scanned all the cages around her.

For now, Nick gave up the search. The internal debate almost gave her a mental breakdown. With the rows of housed animals dominating her attention, it took her a minute to realize someone was shouting her name. A few feet from the exit, she whipped around and saw Natalia coming towards her. Another smaller yet attractive woman followed close behind.

Unconsciously, her mouth stretched into a big goofy grin that had her face hurting by the time both women reached her. She just hoped her awkwardness wouldn't show.

"I didn't expect to see you here." Bobbing her head in greeting.

"I was giving Rachel," Natalia pointed to her right, "a tour of the town. We decided that staying in all day would be a waste. Needless to say, we jumped in the car and just drove."

Nick watched Natalia nibble on her lip and rub her arm. *Is she nervous?*

"So, what are you doing here?"

Words failed her. With her focus on the woman in front of her, she forgot she was even meant to speak. The teeth tugging on full lips stole her attention, drowning out all the other people and sounds around them. Rachel sneezed, bringing her back to the present. Heat rose to her cheeks, and butterflies coiled in her stomach, noticing Natalia staring at her too.

"Bless you," Natalia mumbled to Rachel. Her eyes never wavering.

Remember, she is a client.

"I was contemplating getting a dog," Nick responded.

Her mouth was so dry that it felt like talking through sand.

"But now I'm not so sure. I did, however, see a rabbit and a cat I liked. With me being out of the house a lot and running around, I'm not sure I could care for anything properly."

Why am I telling you all of this?

"So…, Rachel," Regrettably, Nick forced her eyes away to look at Rachel. "Natalia said that you'd be joining us the day after tomorrow. Are you looking forward to it? I think you'll be pleasantly surprised what this town has to offer."

Rachel's eyes bounced back and forth between both women. Nick didn't dare look at Natalia but felt her eyes on her like a flashlight.

"I can't wait." Excitement filled her eyes. "Hopefully, I could get her to decide on something." Leaning a shoulder into her friend, Rachel playfully frowns at Natalia. "She was always so picky."

Natalia lightly smacks Rachel on the arm and sticks her tongue out. Inappropriate thoughts raced through her mind. Lost in naughty visions, Nick missed some of the conversation. Demanding her brain to catch up by blinking a few times, her eyes focused on Rachel, concentrating on her words.

"She wanted to retire early and move here. Now that she's here, it's time for her to get settled."

The sound of her soothing voice, Nick knew she was going to like Rachel. She had a calmness about her that put her at ease.

"It's getting late. I am going to get going. I'll see you gals later then?"

Both women nodded in agreement and Nick said goodbye while turning to walk out. The sun hit her face with dry heat, but the evening wind took the edge off. A wandering mind led to fantasies of Natalia's mouth, but she tried to tap them down. Instead, replacing them with thoughts of the upcoming house hunting. All that ended up doing was creating a mix of both ideas swirling around in her head.

∾

"Could you stare anymore? I mean, you looked as if you wanted to jump on her." Rachel teased.

Snickering ever since they left the shelter. The attraction that she had for Nick was amusing to her friend, and Rachel wouldn't let it go.

"I was not going to jump on her! I was paying close attention to what she was saying." Natalia protested. "Besides what was all that about with the receptionist?" Responding with a raised eyebrow. "You wanted her to take some notes for you."

Bantering back and forth, Natalia saw the corner of Rachel's mouth tilt, and her eyes crinkled at the sides. Telltale signs that her friend was yanking her chain and wouldn't move on till she got some juicy, solid answers.

"We are not talking about me." She said flatly. "Besides, I'm not afraid to admit that I was flirting."

Rachel almost hit the car window as she waved her hands around.

"So, why haven't you asked this Mrs. Ward out on a date yet? The way she was looking at you I doubt she would refuse."

With her focus on the road, Natalia could see Rachel staring at her from the corner of her vision, eagerly awaiting an answer. The last thing she wanted to do was put attention on her own sexual frustration right now. It wasn't an option.

"I barely know her, and who's to say she is even interested in women." Natalia pointed out. "Yes, have thought about asking her out, but this is still a business relationship. I can control myself, unlike some people I know."

Making a point to look at Rachel, she swiftly turned her head and pointedly stared at her for a brief second before placing her attention back on the road.

"My goodness Rachel, I just got out of a mess of a relationship! I don't need anything else right now."

The left turn a little sharper than necessary, both women leaned a bit. Her frustration and anxiety breaking through.

"Calm down. Sorry I pried."

An apologetic tone to her voice.

"I just don't want you to wait too long to get back in the saddle. It's been almost 3 months since the whole Dan fiasco, and I think you deserve a night out."

Rachel shrunk back into the passenger seat. Her tone softer now.

"Even if you just go out to eat - and I don't mean lunch - I mean an actual date where you don't have to think about anything else but the other person sitting across from you, and if you happen to like the person, what's the harm? I just want you to be happy, Nat."

Shifting in her seat, she glanced over at her friend. Arms crossed and brows furrowed, concern and sincerity filled her eyes. The love her friend had for her made her feel a bit remorseful. Blinking back tears to keep them from falling down her cheeks, Natalia tried to maintain focus on the road.

"Let's just get through dinner tonight, and we'll see what happens, okay?"

Pulling to a stop in front of the B&B and cutting the engine. The whispered "OK" that escaped her friend's mouth was so low that she almost missed it. She wondered if Rachel was going through some emotional things and was holding back from her. Nodding her head, Natalia rubbed at her eyes and got out of the car.

Chapter 13

Dinner the night before was great and had their moods improving. The awkwardness of earlier washed away. Everyone curious about Rachel, Natalia almost had to leave her friend at the table and go to bed alone.

Today, Gracie hosted a community barbecue for her guests to comfortably mingle and get to know the town's locals. Smells of cooked meat and burning wood filled the air, making her mouth water. The turnout was hefty, giving Natalia more people to meet. Talking about her work and why she moved, lead her to making promises to go and look at some of the farmer's livestock for consultations. Explaining she was retired didn't hinder her from resisting to help. Rachel beamed a smile and hid a giggle every time she agreed to stop by a home.

One of her many new acquaintances was a local furniture maker. After receiving a business card, he invited her to stop by once she found her new home. Mentioning he would be delighted to help her decide how to decorate.

By the way he behaved throughout the night and stared at some of the guests, Natalia got the inkling she batted for the same team. She found him to be very amusing. Constantly making jokes and trying to pull her into conversations. His infectious humor made her feel welcome and accepted.

After meeting everyone at the cookout at least once, Natalia excused herself and went to sit alone at a table. Closing her eyes to enjoy the peace and quiet. Almost all night, Gracie was right next to Rachel, showing her to one person or another. When it got to be past midnight, and the other guests began to leave, Natalia walked up to Gracie and Rachel to pull her friend away.

After twenty more minutes of small talk, they were finally able to excuse themselves and made their way up to their room. Both women physically and mentally exhausted and as their heads hit their pillow, they fell asleep.

∾

Waking up the next morning, they decided to hang around the B&B for some overdue relaxation. Leisurely consuming breakfast, they got up and made their down to the lake behind the house. A light breeze brought smells of freshly cut grass mingled with dew. A few times, Natalia closed her eyes to breathe in deeply.

Circling the lake, they discussed the clinic back in Tennessee. Their conversation moved to what kind of house Natalia was looking for, the party the night before, and the town. Taking their time catching up and filling each other in. They made several laps and did not touch anymore on her flirtation with Nick, for which Natalia was grateful.

At first, the screeching coming from the distance sounded like a bird to her, but when she started moving towards the sound it became clear it was a dog. With Rachel running behind her, she made her way up to the neighbor's fence. Her lungs burned from her lack of physical exercise, but the sounds of a distressed animal pushed her on.

A black and white collie mix was biting at the wire fence with all its might, only to get stuck even more. The animal lodged underneath the fence tried pulling itself out, but the more the dog moved, the more the wire dug into its flesh.

"Oh my!" Rachel's shaken voice came from behind her. "I'll go grab some wire cutters."

She yelled over her shoulder as she rushed towards the house. The dog began to squirm again, and Natalia eased closer.

"Shhh," She cooed. Trying to calm the dog down so it wouldn't cause any more damage. "Where is your owner? Huh, handsome boy?"

Talking to the frightened animal seemed to be doing the trick. Stilling, it panted raggedly. Looking over the scene, she noted shiny blood covering the wire, making the fur matted and sticky.

"It's ok. You are going to be OK." Attempting to ease some tension as she slowly crept forward. When the dog tried to back away – only to pull at its flesh more – she stopped. Putting her hands out, Natalia kneeled at eye-level with the animal. Pausing, the dog sniffed the air.

In a matter of minutes, Rachel returned with some of the guests from the B&B. The worried look on her face reminded Natalia that staying calm was a priority. Breathing hard, Rachel handed over the wire cutters and a towel. Trying to compose herself, she took a few deep breaths and stood next to her, waiting for more instructions.

Without taking her eyes away from the scared animal, Natalia calmly instructed Rachel. "If you hold the dog down with the towel, I'll cut the wire."

Pausing, she looked around the animal for the best places to start.

"Just be careful." She reminded her. "He is in serious pain and afraid. Please," Pausing again, she scanned the group around them and, in an authoritative tone, said, "Everyone else, stay back. I don't need any accidents."

Closing her eyes, she breathed in through her nose and out through her mouth. Her attempt to saturate some of her nerves.

Calm. Stay calm. You can do this.

She handed Rachel back the towel.

"As soon as the dog gets free, you'll have to keep holding it down while I grab the other end. Then we'll take him up to the car."

Rachel nodded understanding. Being in the same field, she knew Rachel would know what to do. Cautiously, Rachel walked towards the dog. The animal's wide eyes followed her. A low guttural growl sounded. Natalia snapped her fingers to get the animal's attention while Rachel wrapped the towel around the dog's nose in a knot. She held down both ends to the ground.

"Alright, here we go." This type of work was second nature to her; she focused on where the wire gripped the neck and made four cuts. Within seconds he was free.

Not wasting any time, she eased the onlookers aside, and with Rachel's help, they carried the dog up to the car. Normally, Natalia would have the tools with her to take care of the situation, but all her things were in storage. Her only other option, for the time being, is to take the dog down to the ASPCA.

The drive was filled with soft whining noises. A blood-smeared towel covered Rachel's lap in marks as she gripped the dog to keep it still. Mechanically Natalia focused on the drive to the clinic. Her mind not wavering from their task.

The stone building coming into view brought back familiar images from her old practice. Oddly enough, they had similar situations arise there. Before the car came to a complete stop,

Rachel was already opening the car door. Rushing in, they made their way right past a smiling girl at the adoption desk to the Veterinary office.

Evelyn was at the counter. A smile lit up her face when Rachel hurried into the room, only to drop when she realized this wasn't a social visit. Hastily, Rachel explained what happened. With wide eyes, Evelyn buzzed to the back, and two techs hurried out.

They immediately took the wounded animal straight to the back. The doorway showed the techs placing the injured and unmoving dog into a cage. In hushed tones, they mumbled something to one another, nodded, and left the room.

"Dr. Withers is already in surgery right now. Those are her only volunteer technicians." She explained. "They came in to help with the surgery. She should be in soon." Evelyn stood at the door, fidgeting with her hands, looking sullen at the still form in the cage.

Natalia blew out a frustrated breath. "We don't have that kind of time." She motioned at the unconscious animal. "Who knows how long the dog was out there? He already lost a lot of blood." Rachel shuffled her feet next to her. "We've got to clean him up now."

"I'll let the Doctor know that you need her A.S.A.P."

Chewing on a nail, Evelyn pushed off the door and nodded. They watched her scurry away. Scenarios played out in her mind making her unable to wait. Natalia pushed through the door and went to work.

Knowing full well that surgery could take a long time, especially if there is a problem, she didn't want to risk the dog losing more blood.

Without a word, Rachel followed behind her and picked the dog up out of the cage. The fluorescent lights gleamed off the sterile metal exam table. Gently she lowered the dog while Natalia searched for saline. Like old times, they fell into their normal dynamic. Rachel hummed to herself as she worked side by side with her former boss.

After placing the line and administering saline for dehydration, she shaved around the animals' neck to reveal all the puncture wounds. Superficial cuts mixed in with more deep puncture wounds closer to the base of his jaw. Blood loss, dehydration, and exhaustion taxed his body, but soon he started coming too. She breathed a sigh of relief and grabbed a sedative to keep him calm while they worked.

Almost an hour later, the procedure was done, and they began to clean up. Shortly in, Natalia revealed a laceration cut into the jugular vein at the nape of his neck. She worked diligently to repair the vein and control the hemorrhaging.

As she removed her gloves, Rachel placed the dog into one of the recovery cages. A slightly heavy-set man with dark brown eyes and hair that ended just above his eyebrows walked through the door. His expression serious, but slightly softened by the glasses high on the bridge of his nose.

"What's going on in here?" The glasses slid down slightly when he tilted his chin downward. He scanned the room, taking in the sight before him. A humming noise came from his nose, and his mouth hardened into a thin line.

"I heard about a dog with lacerations that required attention." His questioning gaze landed on her own.

"Hi." Natalia began, extending her hand. "I presume you're Dr. Withers."

Taking her hand with a light grip, he shook it. "I'm Dr. Purez. This dog got caught in a wire fence. He had several deep lacerations to his neck. One of them had cut into his jugular vein that I cauterized, along with some artificial ones to his front paws."

Folding his arms, he looked over at the cage with raised eyebrows.

"I stopped the bleeding, cleaned out the wounds, and closed up the ones I could with stitching. One required a drain. Other than that, he should heal pretty well. I do recommend some pain medication and rest"

The corner of his mouth lifted, and he nodded his head. Stepping around her, he knelt down to look at the animal resting on a towel. Its chest rose and fell with ease as it slumbered from the anesthetic medication. A grin showing white teeth greeted them when he turned around.

"Well, it looks like you have everything under control in here. Evelyn said you're a veterinarian from Tennessee?"

Natalia nodded.

"If you want a job, you got one. I know Jake here will be grateful when he's feeling better." His hand waving in the direction of the dog.

"Jake?"

"The dog you saved. His name is Jake. I'd better call Fletcher. He's probably running around everywhere looking for him."

Dr. Withers shakes his head with a small laugh. "He gets out often and I keep telling him to put a tracker on him."

"Um, okay."

Her voice rose a pinch from the surprise as she turned to Rachel, who was grinning.

"Well, I am just glad I was able to help." Tossing her gloves in the hazardous trash bin, she went to the sink to wash off.

"Fletcher will be glad too."

Quickly she washed and dried her hands. Turning back around, she waved at Rachel.

"And thanks, but I am not looking for a job right now. I'm supposed to be on retirement. I'll let you know if I decide to go back to working."

Taking his outstretched hand, she shook it one last time. His frown gave her an odd feeling. Ignoring it, Natalia nodded again and followed Rachel out of the clinic.

The feeling continued as they made their way outside into the evening air. Something itched at her consciousness. With her attention in several directions, she almost ran right into her car.

"Wow, I'm just glad we were there. It felt great being by your side again, Nat."

Rachel, unaware that her friend was distracted, opened her car door and slipped inside.

It did feel great to be helping out. She agreed, sliding into the driver's side.

Before leaving, Natalia called Gracie to inform her what was going on. Some of the guests and locals who had been at the scene had given her a rundown of what they saw, and Natalia filled her in on the rest. Gracie asked if they needed anything in her motherly tone that had Natalia smiling at the concern in the other woman's voice.

∽

With lunchtime approaching, both women found themselves back at the deli they had visited the previous day. Adrenaline pulsed through their systems as they ordered. The calming, personal touches helped Natalia to unwind, and as her heartbeat began to go back to a normal rhythm, she decided this quaint shop would become her daily chow spot.

After an hour of light chatter and filling food, they were headed back to the B&B with full stomachs. The heaviness brought a yawn to her lips, making her movements sluggish with a need for a nap.

Gracie had been scarce all day, surprising Natalia, who usually would see the elderly woman walking about as she cleaned, talking to anyone in her path. Their chat early this morning was the only contact she had made, but she wasn't worried. Natalia assumed Gracie needed a break from the guests.

Rachel suggested they sit on the front porch to watch the sunset. For whatever reason, rocking back and forth and seeing the trees blowing in the wind brought Nick's face to her.

"You're thinking of her, aren't you?" Rachel commented as though she had read her mind. A smile played on her friend's lips. "I have known you long enough to tell when you're daydreaming."

A sigh escaping her, "Yes, I was thinking of her. I couldn't help myself."

A quick look around before her eyes landed on Rachel's. "It's something about the wind." Her chest tightened a little. "It makes me want to share it with her."

The attempted smile faltered at her friend's eye roll.

"I can't help it. I think of her several times a day, and when I see her face, I don't know." An exhale of air emphasized her frustration. "I barely even know her. Do you think I'm going crazy?"

Rolling her head to the side, small cracking sounds could be heard. Rachel shifted to stare back out at the scenery. A faraway look on her face. Her words were soft and comforting.

"You're not going crazy. I think you're lonely, and I can relate."

The honest confession caught her off guard. She opened her mouth, ready to speak, but the words died before she could speak. Rachel didn't notice as she continued.

"I was thinking about moving too. Not for you, but for myself."

She sighed and looked down at her hands. Fidgeting with her nails in her lap.

"I miss having someone next to me all night. Back home, everyone knows everyone, and I keep running into old girlfriends."

Taking in the irony of her words, Natalia bit back a chuckle.

"Having relationships that only last a few weeks at a time doesn't help, and it kind of sucks."

Her hands stilled, and she sighed, sitting up straight to look out at the quiet neighborhood. Natalia's heart ached for her friend. She understood all too well how lonely someone could feel.

"Now that you're gone, I don't have anyone to talk to. Nothing to take up my time or to distract me."

The words, even with the light laugh at the end, had a sullenness to them. Looking out at the setting sun, she blinked a few times. She told herself it was because of the glare in her eyes, but partially it was her holding back the tears pricking her eyes.

"Being at work is like putting on a shoe that's too small. Me and you could just work without even needing to say a word."

Natalia's heart sank a little at the morose demeanor her friend reflected. How could she make her feel better when she couldn't solve the problems she was having.

"We were in sync. Just like today - it comes naturally. This new Doc just keeps barking orders." A harsh tone filled the space between them. "Everyone is either on edge or frustrated. Some of the staff left already."

Turning her head, she noted a frown playing on Rachel's lips, and she clenched her jaw. Natalia knew she struggled with her emotions. Rachel loved

Tennessee. Her life and her family, who were all there, made her heart ache for her longtime friend.

"You should do whatever you feel is best for you. I will never complain about you moving closer to me, but Rachel, if you need to get away, you should."

Speaking the truth, she looked her friend in the eyes.

"If you're having problems at work, you may need to speak to the new Vet. My personal advice would be to get out of the house and meet new people. Get out of your normal comfort zone."

The corners of Rachel's mouth lifted with her next words.

"Maybe this time, find a girl that wants a long-term commitment. Someone with some *morals*. That's what I suggest."

Rachel's mouth opened then abruptly shut when a squeaky motor was heard coming up the road. Watching as Gracie slowly pulled up to the house. Her hair was a bit disheveled, and mumbling to herself when she exited the vehicle. Words silencing when she noticed the two women on the porch staring. The smile she displayed showed wrinkles at the corners while slowly, she made her way up the front stairs.

"Good evening, ladies!" Her cherry voice came out almost in song. "What are you getting into?"

"We were just talking." Natalia stopped rocking. "Haven't seen you all day. Where have you been?"

"I went to see my physician."

Gracie rubbed her arm. Her pace slowed as she reached the top of the stairs.

"I needed to get a tetanus or rabies shot." Her voice rose with her next words. "That ferret gave me a goodbye bite before he left with his family this morning."

Both women laughed at the face Gracie made. More wrinkles showed as she scrunched her face up in disgust.

"It hurt like hell with these old bones. But now it's all taken care of." Shaking her head and dropping her hand, she strode past them and went inside.

"Wow, I didn't expect to hear that. Why would you bring a ferret on vacation?"

Rachel questioned, barely keeping her smirk to herself. The urge to break out in a burst of laughter almost got the better of her.

"I'm not sure." Natalia shrugged. "The little boy didn't want to leave home without it, I guess."

Natalia smiled to herself as she had a memory come to mind.

"She found it the other day in the laundry. I'm guessing it got out a lot."

Both women chuckled at the image.

"She looks like she'll be okay though. Probably scared her more than anything." Smiling, Natalia asked if she was ready for dinner.

"No. I think I'm still full from lunch and dinner the night before."

A low burp escaped, and she rubbed her bloated stomach.

"I'm going to go up to the room and get some rest."

Brushing some dust from her clothes, Rachel slowly stood, stretching out her arms. Natalia nodded, a light creak from the swing as she stood and followed her friend inside their room. The excitement of the day also made her crave early bedtime.

Chapter 14

"I know it's a little early to be calling, but I think I found just the place for you. The only catch is, if you want it, you'll have to make an offer on it by one o'clock, or the bank will take it."

Nick's voice cracked, and she cleared her throat. Anxiety filled her chest over whether or not she should call so early in the morning, but understanding this was time-sensitive, reason outweighed her anxiety.

"This was listed for a possible short sale due to the bankruptcy foreclosure. Before the bank takes possession, they are thinking of placing it up for auction."

Calling at seven in the morning, she expected not to get an answer but was surprised when Natalia picked up. Her groggy voice sent shivers down her spine, causing heated waves to fill her stomach.

"It must be something if you dare to wake one woman let alone two up this early in the morning. You owe me breakfast for this."

Natalia's words, low and husky, made Nick unable to tell if she was actually upset or teasing her. The thought of the ladder made her heart rate sped up. An image of breakfast in bed assaulted her mental task list for today.

"I think I can manage to get you both breakfasts. So, do you think you'll be ready in thirty minutes?" Changing the subject, Nick rushed on before her mind lingered too long.

"I can manage that." A deep yawn filtered through the line. "It'll be interesting waking up Rachel, though. She," a boisterous yawn broke her speech again. "Excuse me… She isn't a morning person."

"Okay, well, try your best. Maybe give her some coffee before you do."

The throaty laugh did naughty things to her core, and Nick quickly squeezed her thighs together.

"That isn't a bad idea."

"Good." Nick bit back a groan. "I'll see you soon."

Without waiting for a response, she ended the call. Nick went and threw on a pair of shorts and a white T-shirt, all the while tampering down the throbbing between her thighs. She hoped she could make it through today without a professional problem.

When her phone rang at six in the morning, she had jumped out of a deep sleep. Stunned that the Olsen's rang her in a panic.

While planning their mother's funeral arrangements, Frank and Julie had heartbreakingly learned about her staggering financial problems. Both of them were at a loss of what to do. Their late mother was amid foreclosure due to a default of a Chapter thirteen bankruptcy her children knew nothing about.

Julie didn't know anyone else to call and ask for advice. Neither she nor her brother wanted to keep the house because they didn't want the burden of the debt. Knowing Nick since infancy, the sibling felt comfortable calling and asking her for her real-estate help.

No sooner had they mentioned listing than Nick's first thought was of Natalia. The property was a perfect fit for what she was in search of.

Julie said they'd be there cleaning out the house all day. With many items to still go through, she was welcome to pop over for a viewing.

Julie's voice broke a few times as they talked of their past. So many memories, both good and bad. Nick's heart went out to both of them. Losing a loved one, let alone a parent was a pain she wished no one would have to feel.

The hum of the engine mingled with the soft purr of the air conditioner as she made her way over to the B&B. The sounds created their own music as buildings and landscapes passed her by.

Images of her life and the people around her danced across her field of vision. Such things usually brought solace to her mood. Instead, her mind took hold of one and ran with it.

Natalia's sensual voice in the early morning depicted how it would be to wake up with her against her side. The visual had Nick gripping the steering wheel, turning her knuckles white.

Her mind begged to see Natalia's hair sprawled out on her bed; her eyes glazed over from sleep. After a night of passionate lovemaking, Natalia would curl up and fall asleep to the sounds of her heart beating. Becoming lost in thought, she almost missed the turn for the B&B.

Natalia and Rachel were standing out front waiting when she pulled in. Sweaty palms slipped off the steering wheel, and inconspicuously, she wiped them on her shorts.

Rachel, in her tan tank top and white Capri pants, resembled any of the other locals. The limited time she has spent here must agree with her. Glancing at Natalia, her tanning skin from being out in the blistering sun gave Nick an overwhelming urge to run her hands across every inch.

Shifting in her seat, she moved her eyes to calm her libido with no luck. Her teal halter top showed off tan arms and brought her breasts to attention.

They are ample, she thought.

Nick's mouth watered immensely, and she had to swallow. Hard.

Rolling down the window, she called them over to climb in. Keeping the place a surprise, she kept the location of the home to herself. Nick knew in her gut that this house was what Natalia had been looking for.

This drive caused a bittersweet feeling in her chest. She was excited to be fulfilling her client's needs but also upset that their time together might be coming to an end. The sour feeling in the pit of her stomach was confusing. She barely knew this woman.

༄

Trying to pry any information about the house out of Nick, was proving to be impossible. Brushing off or completely ignoring parts of the conversation wasn't lost on either woman, and the sly smile creeping up on her face only made it more unbearable. Natalia always likes to know exactly where she is going, with her days planned out and organized. Less room for error when prepared, but giving the reins up to someone she hardly knew, felt like nails on a chalkboard to her psyche.

The lush hills and rolling pastures right outside her window were displayed against a clear blue sky. As they passed, the landscape opened up into a sea of flat lands full of willow trees. A picturesque scene before her, and she closed her eyes for a moment to calm her racing heart.

No reason to get worked up. You hired her to do a job, and she is doing that job.

A few deep breaths before blinking her eyes open against the bright sun. With the rising temperatures, they kept the windows up, but the scenery did have her longing to lay her head on the door, letting the wind blow through her hair.

Getting the urge to ask more questions, Natalia held her tongue as Nick took a left turn down a hidden driveway.

"We're here." Nick's voice rose excitedly, and a smile broke out on her face.

Straightening herself in her seat, both Natalia and Rachel turned to look out their windows. The grass took over the landscape so profusely that the only way to tell there was a road was by the massive oak trees dominating both sides of the blacktop. Beautiful bursting trees guarded the path down the driveway towards the home.

Untamed acres of tall grass swayed in the light breeze, and tiny blades kissed the tires of the car as they drove. Overgrown flat land, a sea of the most beautiful lemon–yellow color of grass Natalia had ever seen.

It goes on forever, she thought to herself.

For a moment, Natalia wondered if they would ever reach the end of the long driveway, but four acres later, they came to a circular end. Pulling up in front of the old white Victorian farmhouse seemed something out of a magazine. Tall, wide, burgundy-outlined windows dressed the house, giving it a homey feel. The colors blended in nicely with matching burgundy shutters and charcoal-colored roof.

The spacious front porch begged for guests. The inviting space large enough for several patio sets. Perfect for a house gathering.

Just what I was looking for to relax and possibly host parties.

Framed by the sereneness of the country, Natalia wondered to herself if this was too good to be.

"And it is less than a half-hour from town," Nick said, putting the car in park.

The doors gave a slight squeak as they all got out at once. Rachel and Natalia were speechless. Taking in their surroundings, Natalia couldn't help the smile playing across her face. She had to admit, she was starting to worry about finding what she was looking for, but this home had her getting her hopes up.

Back in her hometown, nothing came close to this. Gone were the harsh landscapes and gravel trails. Only miles and miles of luscious grass lay before her. Nick stood there, leaning against the driver's side door not saying a word, taking in the women's reactions. Natalia met Nick's gaze and her infectious smile.

"Gorgeous, isn't it?"

Her mouth ran dry as her eyes followed the muscles flexing under Nick's shirt as she stretched.

You have no idea...

Feeling a blush creep into her cheeks, Natalia bit her lip and turned to look back at the house.

"I first saw this house when I was little, and I was taken aback by it too." Nick closed her car door, moving around to where they were. "So, shall we go inside and take a look around?" Smiling, Nick gestured with her for the two women to go on in.

"You don't have to ask me twice." Rachel piped up, making her way towards the front steps.

"Wow, I don't think I have seen anything like this in person." Natalia echoed what was in her mind. "It's as if you took a painting from the history pages and made it come to life. It's absolutely stunning." The pair walked past Nick and proceeded to make their way up the stairs.

"You took the words right out of my mouth! I mean goodness Nat, you'll never find anything like this back in Tennessee."

Rachel expresses her awe for the house by waving her arm around. Creaking steps mirrored their steps as they ascended the porch to the front door. The welcoming sounds give the essence of familiarity. Smells of apples greeted them upon opening the front door.

Both women came to a stop just inside the entrance, causing Nick to swerve to the side or risk running into them. Natalia, acutely aware of this, smiled.

The foyer had a grand oak staircase. Her head tilted back to take in the 10-foot-high ceiling, decorated with a crystal chandelier hanging in the center.

"Damn," Rachel commented.

"I know," Nick spoke from behind them.

Open doorways stood on either side of them in the foyer. The right leads to a family room. Natalia turned her head and made her way slowly around the beautiful open space. The same light oak hardwood flooring beneath their feet, and she suspected it would continue throughout the rest of the house. Against the far-right wall, a brown and grey stone fireplace stood, reaching all the way to the ceiling.

Making their way back to the foyer, they proceeded to the other open doorway. Although empty, the dining room did bring in a lot of light from the big-picture window. Identical to the window in the living room, it showcased a view of the front yard.

Through the dining room, they made their way into the kitchen. Deep cherry cabinets lined the walls. Nick followed behind while Natalia opened cabinets and checked the plumbing. Realizing this may take a moment, Nick stood beside Rachel and watched.

"The black stainless-steel appliances are new and all working," Nick informed them and folded her arms over her chest. "I confirmed it when I spoke to the owners this morning."

"That's good." Rachel nodded, leaning on the chestnut color granite countertops. They glittered with the sunlight shining through the wall of windows to the left of the room, giving the space an illusion of more space.

Noticing another doorway to the right of the kitchen, she casually made her way over to it. Running her hand across the countertops as she went.

"You could use this as a den or bonus room," Nick said behind them.

Natalia nodded, deciding if she bought this house, this was where she would be spending most of her time. Floor-to-ceiling windows covered every wall, bringing in an ample amount of light. Covering her eyes from the almost blinding light, she adored the magical shadows they created from the swaying trees outside. Imagining what it would look like at night with the stars shining through, she let out a sigh.

"This room was a focal point for the family." Nick leaned against the door frame. Natalia turned to watch her as she lovingly looked around the room. A smile, not yet reaching her eyes, came over her face.

"I bet it was," Natalia replied. Their eyes met, and tiny sparks filtered between them. For the briefest of moments, she had an image of them together in this space before Nick broke eye contact.

"Think of all the parties you could have Nat," Rachel said sarcastically from the wall of windows. Natalia laughed as she made her way over to her friend.

Mature willow trees mixed with other adult trees, littering the property, giving the perfect balance of shade and sun across the yard.

"Parties are not as much my thing as they are yours, Rachel." Natalia teased.

"True. True."

"Should we continue looking?" Nick suggested. Both women turned and nodded.

Heading back, they found another door leading to a screened-in porch. The room big enough to fit a coffee table and some lounge chairs. A good spot for breakfast.

A soft buzzing filled the room.

"What is that?" Rachel asked.

Shrugging, Natalia looked around the room. Nick jumped and pulled out her phone.

"Excuse me." Waving her hand, "I need to take this." Tapping her screen, she made her way out of the room.

"Hmmm…" Rachel turned to her, raising an eyebrow.

Shrugging again, Natalia dismissed the odd look Rachel gave her and turned her focus to the landscape. Staring out at the backyard from the porch, Natalia was amazed to see a fair-sized red barn with two fenced-in pastures side by side.

"Both of those pastures are around 5 acres each," Nick commented from the hallway, startling her before returning to mumbling into her phone again.

Observing the structure further, Natalia noticed the slight decline toward the far end of each pasture. The only difference was that the right one had a pond at the bottom of the decline.

"It's everything I imagined." She whispered to herself. "I never thought I'd find it."

It's just perfect. Her thoughts an echo of her feelings.

"But you did, Nat. I guess that's why they say 'patience is a virtue'." Jumping at the unexpectedness of Rachel's words, she swung around. Rachel gave her a funny look, but as she opened her mouth to respond, Nick came into the room asking their thoughts.

"It's beautiful." Her words were automatic and heartfelt. "It seems almost too good to be true. I can't believe they would even want to sell it."

"Yea.... what is the catch?" An edge of disbelief filled Rachel's tone.

"The owner passed away," A brief pause as a sad expression filled Nick's features. Blinking a couple of times, she straightened herself.

"The family doesn't want to keep it. They are accepting offers if you are interested."

Natalia wanted to ask more, but prying wasn't her forte. Hating it when people would try to push themselves into her affairs. She wasn't going to do that to someone else.

"Have you checked out the upstairs yet?" Her voice more professional, pointed behind her.

"No, I haven't." Figuring Nick didn't want to talk further about the situation. "I guess I should go take a look."

Turning her head to nod at Rachel, she mumbled under her breath realizing her friend had left already to go upstairs. Anticipation and shyness hummed through her. Feelings became too intense and she dropped her eyes to the floor.

"Well, come on then." Nick bent towards her, taking her hand to lead her to the stairs. Warmth flooded her. All Natalia could think was how perfectly their hands fit together. Their entwined fingers sent delicious shivers up her arm and gave her a jolt of confusing energy.

Nick squeezed her hand, tugging her along. Focusing, Natalia willed her heartbeat to slow down. Allowing Nick to lead her to the staircase, she assumed Nick would let go of her hand when they reached it, but she never did. If anything, she held on a little tighter.

She was unable to relish over the feelings stirring inside her for too long because as soon as they reached the top of the stairs, Rachel's voice came from one of the many rooms. An icy chill caused her to frown when Nick dropped her hand.

Chapter 15

Drawing in a sharp breath of air didn't abate the stinging disappointment the sudden loss of contact created. Rachel called out from the other room, and Natalia pushed her sullen mood aside. Without a word, Nick placed a hand on the swell of her back, silently leading her into the other room.

The thudding of her heart drowned out much of what was being said around her. Her body hummed as her mind raced. This day brought about so many new opportunities, but she didn't believe it could get any better. Standing in her dream home, with the woman she had been fantasizing about for a few weeks now, was touching her. Solid and sure hands made her skin burn like it was on fire. Goosebumps broke out along her arms. The contact only solidified her need for more.

Rachel's bubbling voice and waving arm interrupted Natalia's wandering thoughts. Trying to keep up with her tangent about decorating the master bedroom proved difficult. The words were not registering all the way. Instead, they still wandered to more intimate thoughts as Nick's hand rubbed her back lightly.

"Mmmhmm." She mumbled at one of Rachel's comments.

Smiling, she nodded. Her eyes followed Rachel as she walked about the room. Nick's hand moved further up her spine, and a shiver broke through her. Glad that Rachel hadn't noticed, Natalia turned slightly to look behind her.

Nick's eyes followed Rachel, commenting on the view when her eyes shifted towards hers. She smiled and gave Natalia a wink. Heat rose to her cheeks, and her stomach flipped as Nick dropped her hand from her back.

"What do you think, Nat?"

"What?"

"What do you think of changing the paint color?"

Shaking her head and running a hand through her hair, Natalia shifted her focus from Nick's alluring smile and turned toward her friend.

"Oh, right. I agree it could use some, but I wouldn't want to take away from the view of the room."

Rachel frowned and looked out the window again. Taking a moment, Natalia mentally calmed herself down before moving to stand next to her friend. The feeling of eyes on her had her fighting the urge to turn around.

"You're right." Rachel crossed her arms. "But I still think it needs more color." Her eyes scanned the room again before looking back outside. "All the white is a bit bland."

Chuckling, Natalia's shoulder bumped into her friend. "Maybe some light color, but the view is what matters."

"And it is stunning," Nick said from behind them.

Rachel just smiled and nodded in agreement, but the low, husky tone was not lost on her. Instant tingles spread through her body at the meaning behind those words.

"This home was made to take advantage of the landscape." Casually continuing when both women turned to look at her. "The big picture windows offer plenty of light and are double paned for great insulation."

"Hey," Rachel turned to look at Natalie, "One less thing to add to your 'fix-it' list." She chuckled before leaning forward and opening the latches to lift the window.

A struggling breeze came into the room as the sill creaked open. Natalia breathed in a shallow breath of warm air. Spans of greenery filled her vision. Sun filtered through all the trees, splashing the room in specks of glittering light, giving the room a mystical fairytale essence.

"I bet it gets a lot of good circulation at night, too." Commenting on the soft wind flowing into the room.

The natural beauty of the landscape, Natalia would never have a reason to put blinds up. The light hitting her skin warmed her, mimicking the feeling of Nick's hand in hers. The memory of their skin touching had her wondering if all of her was just as soft.

Before continuing her train of thought, Rachel gripped her arm and led her into the enormous master bathroom.

"Whoa."

The words from Rachel were the same ones floating in her head. Her eyes traveled the room, taking in all the fixtures.

"Could you imagine bathing in this?"

Natalia shook her head. "Anyone could watch you. Why is there no surround? At least a curtain?"

Expressing her concerns out loud, taking in the cast iron claw foot tub resting in front of floor-to-ceiling bow windows that openly looked out over the backyard.

"I think that is the point. They obviously are not shy." Sarcastically laughing at the obvious. Natalia wasn't amused.

A low chuckle came behind her near the doorway, and she shook her head in response.

Not my kind of thrill.

On the opposite wall, stunning dual sinks set into black and white granite countertops. They lined the wall like a painting. The color scheme continued into the shower stall that occupied the other corner of the room.

Sweeping her gaze about the room, she imagined herself living in the space. The shower would get used more than the bath unless she did something about the window view.

The first thing on my to-do list?

"What do you think?"

Rachel spun around and answered first. "I think I am jealous. This is awesome!"

The soft chuckle made her smile, and Natalia turned around to see Nick watching her. Her nerves got the better of her, and she swallowed and bit the inside of her lip.

Nick's eyes dropped to watch the motion, and heat pooled deep in her stomach. With her eyes still fixated on her mouth, Nick responded with, "The windows make the space."

A whimper almost escaped when Rachel attached to her arm again.

"Well, next room."

Unknowingly saving her from embarrassing herself, she allowed her friend to pull her away. Easily bored, Rachel steadily moved her from room to room to room. In each new space, Rachel would comment about random aspects of the home, while Natalia simply nodded her head, making short assessments, but her mind wouldn't stop wandering.

Further down the landing was another guest bedroom with an on-suite. They briefly viewed it and then moved to the final two nice-sized rooms with a Jack and Jill bathroom. All the rooms were void of furniture, leaving bare hardwood floors, which echoed as they moved about the room. The last room also had wonderful views of the willow trees and the pond out back.

Impatient, Rachel suggested they go look at the barn out back. Still getting a feel for the room's layout, Natalia told her to go ahead without her- assuring her she'd catch up a little later.

Too many options, she thought as she mentally designed what this room could be. Alone with her thoughts, she found herself unable to relax. Endless decisions mingled with conflicting emotions, causing her to become distracted.

Unexpectedly, all the hair on her body stood at attention. Hot breath brushed the nape of her neck, stirring the whisps of hair around her face. A familiar scent encircled around her, and she was acutely aware of the heat radiating off Nick's body as she pressed into her back. The energy in the room swelled. Thick and heavy with electricity, her heart beat against her ribs. The racing skipped a beat when Nick placed her hand around her waist.

Firm fingers gripped her hip, pulling her backward, and all her thoughts evaporated. Tenderly, her hair was brushed aside, revealing the creamy, lush skin of her neck. Instinctively, Natalia let out a soft noise and rolled her neck. Wetness rushed between her legs, and her breath stilled in her chest. Millions of butterflies swarmed her stomach and had her biting back a giggle.

A whispered sigh escaped as Nick's lips seared her skin, invisibly marking her and making her clit twitch. A noise, reminding her of a snarl, vibrated against her neck. Her nipples hardened, rubbing against the fabric of her shirt. A moan escaped at the friction, and her body screamed out for more contact.

Fingers dug into the fabric at her waist, and she involuntarily rubbed her bottom into the front of Nick's pants. The noises filling her ears had her rubbing harder. Grabbing a handful of loose hair, Nick firmly tugged.

Natalia let out a husky moan as more of her skin was feasted on. Barely able to stand it any longer, she snaked her hands up and curled them into Nicks strands. Intending to turn around and steal a kiss, she licked her lips.

Just above a whisper, Nick breathed into her ear, "You're too beautiful."

Natalia froze. A bucket of ice had been thrown on her libido with the sound of those three words. Unwanted memories crashed down on her, shattering the perfect bubble she had been encapsulated in.

～

"You think you're too beautiful! Well, you are too beautiful!" Words hissed out. "I'm tired of always being compared to you! I always think I'm not good enough for you; it makes me sick and depressed. I can't stand being in a relationship where I'm always second best!" Wildly, hands flailed around. "That's why it is so hard to be with a woman, especially one who doesn't care about her so-called other half!"

Words spit out at her like bullets. Every one of them stung as they pierced her soul.

"I did care about you!" Natalia screamed back. "I always will!" Her voice choking on a sob. "But you are right. It's hard being with someone who doesn't care about their other half!"

The words ripped at the inside of her throat like a band-aide. The pain accompanied by relief. It was an understanding of resolve that this was the finality of them.

"It's always been about you and never about me." Tears pricked at the edges of her vision. Angrily, she blinked them away. The sadness was overshadowed by the rising rage filling her tone.

"I can't help it if I'm attractive, Dan." The rolling of her eyes matched her flat bravado. "You used to say that's what caught your eye in the first place, and now you're bashing me for it. You never once said it was a problem before!"

Dan looked at her with irritation. The tilt of her mouth made Natalia want to slap her.

"You're the one trying to get me to wear the clothes YOU buy me."

Dan crossed her arms at the emphasized word. The action made more emotion pool deep in her stomach.

"They barely cover up a thing! And if you think you're second best, it's because you've made it so."

Unfolding her arms, Dan scowled. Shaking her head, she opened her mouth to speak but snapped it shut when Natalia cut her off.

"Always trying to show me off to your friends like I'm some sort of trophy for you. It's disgusting."

Natalia ignored the flexing of Dan's jaw. She knew it was a sign of her impatience.

"I never wanted to go to those parties," An overwhelming feeling settled into her chest as she continued. "But you always insist and get mad when I tell you I'm staying home." Unable to control the shrill whine at the end of her sentence proved her inability to hold herself together.

"Still goes to show that you don't give a damn about what I feel. You never have."

Moving closer, Dan's words sprinkled little droplets of spit at her as she yelled. Their eyes locked, and for a moment, Natalia thought she might hit her.

"I try to give you nice things and do things for you, and all you do is throw it back in my face. When I ask you to forgive me for one little thing... ONE. LITTLE. THING. Could you help me? No! You reject me."

Natalia's breath caught in her throat when Dan's fist clenched at her sides.

"You couldn't do just the simple task of loving me!"

The closeness had her scream ringing in her ears. The vibration intensified the growing headache she had.

"That means all of me. The good and the bad. The new and the old. You couldn't just let go and love me! So now, you think you'll just leave me?!"

Balling and unbaling her fist, she let out a horrible scream before turning and taking a few steps away. Natalia watched her as she paused, seemingly taking a few breaths. Her back rose and fell like her panicked heartbeats. With wide eyes, she watched Dan's head tilt back to face the ceiling. Another scream bellowed out into the air.

"No!" She lowered her head and swiveled around to face her.

"Fuck you!"

The words flew from her dry mouth. Her cheeks flushed red as she quickly made long strides to stand toe to toe with her again.

"That's all you can do is leave." Dan's flushed face was painted with dry tear streaks.

How dare she say that she yelled in her mind. The main reason for all of this was because of her actions. Hers! Rage twisted in her gut at all the accusations of her loyalty that she felt like exploding. "I did love you!" This time the shrill uncontrollable. The high pitch of her voice cracked with her anger. "I don't know what you expect of me! Yes, I'm leaving this house. But you left this relationship a long, long time ago."

Hands fell to her sides as her mind reeled at the audacity. The adrenaline rush of rage now waning, as her body became increasingly tired, her anger gave way to relenting sorrow.

"I could tell when it started going bad," Natalia said in an almost whisper. The steeliness of her tone was gone. *"But I stayed trying to mend it."*

Dan took a step backward and crossed her arms. Natalia's face fell at the realization that none of this really mattered anymore.

"I can see now that I never meant anything to you."

Dry, red eyes met hers, and a chill ran through her. She tampered it down.

"It wasn't me who didn't love you. It was you who couldn't love me." As the words spilled out, cognizance of the toxicity of their relationship became clear. *"You couldn't put yourself aside for someone else. I can see that now."*

Natalia crossed her arms, hugging herself, trying to fold into herself. *"Which is why I still can't understand why you'd want to have this baby. You don't know how to give a piece of yourself to another person, let alone give up yourself. You won't be able to handle it."*

Heavy breathing echoed around them. With a bright red face, Dan stepped closer. Her hot breath beat down on Natalia's face.

"Why do you care anyway? You're leaving, remember? Just go if you are going! Go! Get out of here! You're worthless!"

Turning, Natalia walked out of there with Dan screaming at her backside. Nightmares continue to haunt her.

Chapter 16

Sensing the sudden change in her body, Nick backed away. Standing in the afternoon glow of the sun, Natalia's rigid frame mimicked the air around them. From a distance, Nick surveyed her. Taking stock of her unmoving form. To her, it was apparent that something had shifted between them.

Concern danced with caution as Nick slowly made her way around the beautifully still creature in front of her. Her breath caught at the unfocused, darkened eyes that glistened. The need to comfort her was almost overwhelming.

"Is everything okay?" She asked, taking a step toward her. Softly, she asked, "Did I say something or do something to upset you?"

Mentally chiding herself for causing this reaction, Nick refrained from reaching out when a tear fell down her cheek. Unsure it would be welcome, Nick fidgeted with her hands, conflicted about whether she should touch her or leave her alone.

Shaking her head, Natalia wiped at her cheek. Blinking back the unshed tears, she hoarsely replied, "I'm fine. There's really no need to worry."

Right. That only made her worry more.

With a low sniffle, followed by some more blinking, she continued, "I should be catching up with Rachel. She'll be wondering what is taking so long."

Dropping her eyes to the floor, she grazed past Nick. Alone in the silent room, Nick furrowed her brows, pondering what had happened.

I was so stupid. Stupid, stupid, stupid! she yelled to herself.

Frustrated, she ran a hand through her hair as she paced back and forth.

I'm not sure what happened, but whatever it was, I know it's my fault, she concluded. *I just needed to be near her and touch her so badly.*

Placing her hand over her face, she screamed. The noise muffled but still echoed in the vacant room. The small release partially helped to clear her guilty conscience before going in search of her client.

By the time Nick found both women near the barn, she had decided to apologize. No matter what the reason, her touching her had shifted something, and she would take responsibility for it. If Natalia had let her get a word in edge-wise, she would have already said she was sorry.

Approaching them, Natalia wasted no time telling Nick she was ready to go. Shifting her gaze to the ground before her, Natalia ignored Rachel's comments and nudged past both women to go to the car.

"Is there something that happened earlier?"

Taking her focus away from the woman walking through the grass, Nick turned her attention to Rachel. Picking up the concern in her voice as worry painted across her features.

"I mean, she seems so agitated."

"I'm not even sure exactly what happened," Nick stated, not trying to give too much away while her mind still guilt-tripped her. "I don't know what exactly I could have said to make her this upset, but apparently, I must have."

Frowning, Rachel looked past her. Turning, Nick's eyes followed in the same direction.

Without looking at her, she asked, "Could you at least let her know I'm sorry for everything?"

"You sure you don't want to do that yourself?"

Nick sighed. *I would if she would talk to me.*

Still confused, Rachel agreed.

"Thank you." She said, turning to face her. From the questioning look in her eyes, Nick knew she wouldn't let it go. "I appreciate it."

"Sure... no problem."

A sigh of relief, knowing- at least for now- she wouldn't have to explain.

A horn sounded in the distance, making both women jump in response. Her heart leaped in her chest, and in unison, both women blew out a breath.

"We should get going before she leaves without us." Rachel's mouth formed a thin line that told Nick she wasn't joking.

In silence, they made their way up the hill to the house. Deep in thought, her mind raced, still trying to sort out what happened. Although the trek to the car wasn't long, she still felt winded when she reached the driver's side door. Natalia looked distracted, but Nick knew she was more than likely trying to ignore her. That notion got under her skin more than she cared to admit.

Driving back was agony. The attempted small talk was incredibly strained, that turning on the heater on this humid day would have been a meager welcome. The air got thicker by the passing minutes as the awkwardness peeked on unbearable.

The mood, like the silence in the car, filled the space like a wet blanket. All Natalia wanted to do was stare at the passing scenery, and Nick wished she could be privy to her thoughts. Her need to reach in the seat behind her and squeeze her thigh in a reassuring gesture, but she knew that would only cause more drama.

The car pulled to a stop with a slight jerk. She hadn't meant to break as hard, but her body's reaction time was understandably off. Idling in front of the B&B, Nick turned to face Natalia.

"Natalia," Nick began, "I need to know if you're interested in the house." Praying that she would at least talk to her about the house. " I only have a little time left to make them an offer."

Holding her breath, she watched in the rearview mirror as Rachel unbuckled her seat belt and opened the car door.

"Oh, right."

The whispered reply had her focus moving to Natalia. Rachel paused in the open door.

"Well, I am interested in it." Nodding her head, she unbuckled her seat belt, avoiding eye contact. "Write up the offer and come by for me to sign it."

Rachel let out a tiny squeal of excitement, and Nick couldn't help but smile. Her stomach may be in knots right now, but Rachel's mood was infectious.

"Whatever you think would be fair is good."

"OK. Great. I can stop over later." *If you really want me to.* Still unsure of where they stood and not letting go of her selfish behavior earlier, Nick couldn't deny she felt hope that she wanted her to still come over. That hope was a bit tampered as Natalia still would not return her gaze.

"Thank you for showing us around today."

" Yea. It was a good find." Rachel agreed, stepping out of the car. "Well, I guess we will be seeing you soon." Her hand gave a small salute before closing the door.

"You're welcome." Her tone sincere. "I'll be by a little later with the papers."

Nick's heart skipped as the corner of her mouth lifted in a grin.

Damn, she is beautiful.

From the corner of her eye, she nodded at Nick. "See you then.", she replied, opening her door and stepping out into the humid air.

With the shutting of the car door, Nick watched her make her way towards the front porch. All Nick could do was stare at her backside and hope everything would be okay.

Sighing, she put the car back into drive. Driving away felt wrong; Nick never liked leaving things unresolved. It was not in her nature. Playing the afternoon over and over again in her mind drove her mad. She needed to know what went wrong. She needed clarity.

She knew Natalia had felt the same way she did. The reactions of their bodies did not lie. The energy she felt when they were around each other was undeniable. So, what drove her away?

Chapter 17

"Okay, I'm no psychic, buuuut," Drawing out the word, attempting to gain Natalia's attention. "I know something was going on. You gonna tell me or what?"

Standing in the doorway of the hotel room, arms crossed, Rachel waited for her to answer. Reminding Natalia of when she was a stubborn child trying to get answers from her mother. Even in her sullen mood, she couldn't help but laugh at her friend.

"Can't I just say nothing, and we drop it? That would be so much easier at this point."

The corner of Rachel's mouth perked up the tiniest bit, taking the sting out of her appearance. The stern look dissipates as her arms drop to her sides.

Natalia waved her arms in the air. "Or, at least, could you come inside? I don't want to blab my whole story to everyone. This is my town now, and things get talked about."

Emphasizing her words with more hand gestures. "Rumors could make or break some people." Natalia backed up into the room and sat down on the bed, waiting for her friend to come join her.

Judging from the casual display of closing the door and walking over to the bed, Natalia knew her friend was ready to listen. Calmly, she closed her eyes and took a deep breath.

"OK. So," Opening her eyes, she confided everything to her friend. Close to twenty minutes later, her story finished, she sat there staring at her entwined fingers. Nervous about Rachel's reaction to what went on, she stared at her hand in her lap.

The defending silence made her skin itch as she sat on the soft mattress. Watching the nuts and bolts in her friend's head spinning, she felt unease settling in her stomach. Slowly, Rachel reached over and took her hand, stopping her internal contemplation.

"I'm no expert."

Natalia looked up to see Rachel staring straight ahead, seemingly reviewing the wall. Her eyes were moving around a bit, and she blew out a breath before shifting her gaze toward her.

"But the way you just explained how you felt, I can see you are starting to really care for Miss Ward."

Swallowing down a lump in her throat, she was going to protest, tell her that this was all crazy, but Rachel didn't give her that chance.

"I could tell that she also has an interest in you."

Natalia sat up straighter. *What?*

"Giiirll, there a lightning bolt that shot between the two of you. As much as you kept telling me how professional you needed to keep this, you can't fight an attraction that strong."

Getting up to stretch, Rachel let out a big yawn. Turning back around, she firmly placed both hands on either side of Natalia's shoulders and looked her in the eyes. The deep pools held no shame or criticism. Only sympathy and compassion. Her caring ability warmed her heart, causing another lump to form in her throat.

"Okay." Her shoulders eased, and she cleared her throat. "I - I can admit I am attracted to her."

The words flat but precise. Lifting her eyebrows, she stared harder at her. Uneasy, Natalia averted her eyes.

"Okay, okay! Maybe a *big* attraction to her, but I still can't do this." Shrugging Rachel's hands off her, she rolled her shoulders. "It seems wrong for so many rational reasons."

Running her hands down her face, she groaned. 'I mean, we haven't even finished the sale of the house yet." A headache began to form, and she pinched the bridge of her nose. "I do still have to work with her to accomplish that."

Rachel straightened, folded her arms, and lightly tapped her foot.

"I still don't know her that well," Natalia explained. "Plus, what am I supposed to do about the memories that keep returning? If I can't get over what happened with Dan, how am I supposed to give myself to another person?"

Slumping forward on her knees, Natalia rested her head in her hands. Conflicting feelings ran around inside her. Couple that with the angel and demon playing badminton back and forth on her shoulders, and she was at wit's end.

"You need to give yourself a break! For goodness' sake, I'm not saying marry the woman!" Rachel's words pierced her jumbled consciousness. "I'm just saying see where it goes. At least we now know she likes women."

Mentally agreeing with that, she hiccupped a laugh.

"You do need to get over what happened with Dan. It was a long time coming."

Unable to argue with that, she frowned. "We did always feel like apples and oranges," she stated.

"I'm sorry it happened, but it happened, so let it go." Rolling her eyes with her frustration. "If it bothers you that much, why don't you just explain it to the woman? That way, she'll at least know why you reacted the way you did."

"I don't think I'll feel comfortable talking about it." Insecurity over her emotions starting to get the better of her.

"Get over it, Nat," Rachel huffed, "We all have baggage."

The room phone ringing had both women jumping to their feet. An unease filled her stomach when Rachel went to answer it. She hadn't chewed on her nails since she was young, but she had an urge to. The peeling feeling always seemed to give a false satisfaction of calm until she did it too short, and they would bleed. She stared at her nails briefly but looked up before she could bring them to her mouth. On her way back, Rachel patted Natalia on the shoulder.

"Your knight in shining armor is back for you." Laughing at her joke, Rachel walked right past her towards the bathroom.

"Ha ha, very funny." Natalia mocked. Rolling her eyes again, she nodded her head towards the door. "Aren't you coming?"

A sliver of light shone through the cracked bathroom door. "No. I think you can handle this all on your own. I'm taking a shower."

A smirk adorning her face a second before disappearing behind the door. The click of the latch gave the final word. Mentally replaying their conversation, Natalia hustled up the courage to make her way down the stairs.

∽

Every step down the stairs calmed her nerves more and more. Reaching the last step, she finally started to breathe normally again, and then she walked onto the screen porch. The sight of Nick sent her senses into overdrive. The scent of her lilac perfume floated to her from across the room.

Was she wearing that earlier?

Head down, hunched over, Nick was intently reading paperwork. Oblivious to anything around her, Natalia took the time to study her. Strawberry blonde hair was tucked behind her ears. The tint predominantly blonde, probably from being in the sun too much lately.

Even hunched over her paperwork, her shoulders relaxed as her hands moved over the forms. Her mouth moved slightly as her eyes scanned, and Natalia smiled to herself at the similar motions that she would do as she read medical forms.

Sitting back in her chair, Nick blew a strand of hair from her face. Her demeanor more at ease now compared to earlier. Nick's chest rose and fell slowly. It was similar to watching the cattle graze over the pastures back in Tennessee—the motion its own graceful dance.

Those eyes.

The moment Nick looked up; their eyes locked. The mirror of conflicting emotions caught her a bit off guard. The smile she was greeted with didn't fully meet her eyes, and she had another pang of guilt at their earlier interaction.

The shine of Nick's eyes became darker before shutting them. The sudden change had Natalia taken aback.

What was that?

When Nick opened her eyes again, the intense dark green had given way to a pale moss. A shudder flowed through her. Unnoticed, Nick waved for her to come over, pulling out a chair. Smiling back, she made her way over and took the offered seat.

A half-hour passed. A slight headache formed behind her eyes; Natalia attributed it to looking over numerous papers. After signing the offer, Nick quickly gathered them up and packed up her things.

Holding out her hand, Natalia shook it. "I will get these over, and I will let you know what steps are next."

What should have been a cheerful, joyous moment felt off. The words died off into silence, and they stood there. Their hands still clasped but not moving.

Noting the awkward moment, Nick nodded, dropped her hand, and turned to leave. Pausing with her back to her, Nick mumbled something under her breath before swiveling back around to face her. A hard knot formed in the pit of Natalia's stomach at the expression on her features.

"So, about this morning… I'm sorry if I offended you in any way."

Shoulders slumping forward, Nick gripped the strap of her bag and shifted on her feet.

"I-I couldn't seem to help myself. If you don't want me working with you anymore, I'll understand."

A burning sensation filled her chest at the remorse spilling out of her words. Not wanting to divulge her past, Natalia swallowed the anxiety and gained the courage to explain.

Taking in a deep breath, she scanned the empty room. Thankful no one was around, she took a few steps forward to stand before Nick. Making sure she was looking into her eyes as she spoke.

"When I came out here, the goal was to find a house. So, this…" she motioned between them, "Is unexpected. Honestly, I don't know what I want."

Nick's eyes bulged with surprise and hope, warming Natalia. "I am attracted to you. Very attracted to you, and I am unsure what to do about it."

Nick bit her lip, making Natalia's body react. Clearing her throat, she tried to get the rest of the words out. "I don't want it to get in the way of what we are trying to accomplish right now."

Nick nodded her head in agreement.

"I'm not even sure if I'm ready to jump back in the saddle," Natalia confessed.

"I can understand that," Nick said. Natalia frowned. "But I am still confused about what happened. You seemed like you were interested in me. I mean, you said you were attracted to me. I wasn't imagining it."

Natalia wished she could give a better explanation, but she still wasn't sure how to.

"One minute, you were fine, and then the next, you froze. Your whole demeanor changed in an instant."

A wrinkle line appeared across her forehead as she clasped and unclasped the strap of her bag. A heaviness weighed in Natalia's chest.

"Was it something I did?" Concern painted across Nick's face. Nick wanted answers – no, needed answers, and she wasn't able to give them to her yet.

Natalia clenched and unclenched her hands. The need to chew at her nails increased every second, and she needed to distract herself.

"I'm sorry. It wasn't anything *YOU DID*. Rather what *YOU SAID*."

She watched Nick freeze her shuffling. She tilted her head to the side and crinkled her brows together. It made Natalia want to laugh, but she knew now wasn't the time.

"When you told me I was 'too beautiful', it just brought back some bad memories."

Rubbing her upper arms, Natalia released a shudder. Nick took a step toward her.

"I had a really bad breakup a few months ago. I guess... I'm still not fully over it."

Grabbing her hand, Nick pulled a surprised Natalia towards her. The skin of her hands, so soft and warm, sent goosebumps along her arms. Memorized, Natalia gave in to being pulled towards those green eyes. The welcome they provided made her want to live there.

"I can understand where you're coming from. We all have had bad and good times, but if you let the bad outweigh the good, then what's the point?"

Her vision rested where Nick's fingers laced over hers. For a split second, she wondered if she was capable of letting all the hurt go.

"I would like to give us a shot." Nick squeezed her hand, and Natalia smiled up at her. "Even if it's just a casual dinner. I just want to get to know you. No commitments or promises. Just two women seeing where things go."

Natalia's mouth parted as Nick brought their twined hands to her lips, her eyes never moving from hers. The feathery kiss made - not only her heart - but her insides melt a little.

"Please think that over while I go run this to the Olsen's."

With a wink, Nick released her hand. The loss left a coldness that she despised.

"I have to get this over there soon, or you won't have a shot at it. See you in a few."

Another wink, accompanied by a wicked grin, made Natalia speechless. Her eyes glued to Nick's backside as she walked out of the room, leaving Natalia to ponder over this revelation.

Chapter 18

What a day. Could this be any more surreal?

The Olsen's were relieved to receive the offer. They cried at being able to move on. The release of overwhelming amounts of stress had Nick tearing up right along with them.

Coming back, the offer signed and ready to go, Nick assumed it would be an awkward meeting. Her nerves were on edge until Natalia asked her out to dinner tonight. The only stipulation is that – whatever this is - we take it slow. There would be no argument from her. She looked forward to any time she got to spend with her.

Natalia clarified that this dinner would be a celebration and a way to get to know each other one-on-one. Understanding why Natalia acted a little off eased some of the whiplash of emotions. Even in her confused state, she was willing to get all the weeds out of the way to see how this relationship could flourish.

Before going home, Nick called the bank and informed them of the contract. Faxing all the information over stopped the foreclosure proceedings. After finishing setting up appointments for the home and termite inspection, she quickly went over a mental checklist.

A good thing about small towns is that she could book them both pretty fast and was able to schedule both inspections on the same day to avoid prolonging the process. Both agreeing to come out the day after tomorrow gave Nick a sense of pride. Hopefully, everything goes well, and they will be going to settlement in two weeks as planned.

Now that all the paperwork was completed, she focused on her most significant problem, trying to figure out what to wear. Unsure if this was more of a date or a get-together, she pulled out several different styles of clothes. Smiling to herself, she looked forward to getting to know Natalia more intimately. Hoping to pursue the connection between them.

She realized two things after going through her closet several times within two hours. First, she needed to expand her wardrobe, and second, she loved the color red. Scanning her clothes a final time, Nick settled on a red V-neck blouse and light tan slacks with matching sandals. Laying out her clothes, she quickly showered, got dressed, and pulled her hair back into a clip.

The drive to the next town over was filled with her inner monologue. Scenes of what she expected filled her, reminding her not to scare the gorgeous woman off this time. *Adrian's Reserve* is an Italian restaurant that Nick only visited on occasion.

Walking in, Nick briefly felt concerned that Natalia might have gotten lost with her jumbled directions. She wasn't always the best at explaining locations.

Ironic that I am a realtor… Ha!

Visions of being new in town crossed her mind but diminished when she saw her sitting at a booth against the back wall. Tables crammed full of people filled the room, making her path through the space mimic a maze. Weaving and bobbing so as not to bump into other patrons. She apologized to a waiter who narrowly escaped her elbow.

Finally reaching the table, she greeted the beautiful creature across from her before taking a seat.

"So, you didn't have any trouble finding the place?"

Swallowing a sip of her drink, "Not at all. The directions you and Gracie gave me made it easy enough."

Ah, Gracie.

"This place seems like a good hang-out. It got really busy, real fast."

"It's a popular place with the locals." Nick scanned around the room. "I'm just glad that you didn't get lost."

Leaning over, she lightly rubbed Natalia's hand. For a brief second, their eyes met. The heat between them was tangible. A light shade of pink crept into Natalia's cheeks, and she pulled away.

Maybe she is just as timid as I am?

"Shall we order?" Sitting up, Nick picked up the menu in front of her. "I'm starving."

briskly nodding, the woman across from her picked up her menu too. Her shirt, pulling snugly against her chest, had Nick's mouth running dry.

"I also finished setting up your appointments for the day after tomorrow." She swallowed, "so you shouldn't have a problem going to settlement in two weeks."

The menu gave Nick an escape from staring, providing her hands a distraction from reaching across the table and running her fingers through her thick hair. Although her mind was playing over what she would love to be doing at this very moment, she couldn't ignore Natalia's delicate fingers, nimbly tugging and fidgeting with her orange polo while attempting to read her menu.

Relaxing her shoulders, she focused on calming her breathing. Knowing she wasn't the only one nervous about where this night might lead gave her an odd satisfaction. She wasn't in this alone.

"I am starving too," she said, placing a loose strand of hair behind her ear. "To be honest… it was Rachel's idea we come out tonight."

Piquing her interest, Nick peered over her menu.

"Oh?" A line creased her forehead.

Natalia nodded. "She feels that I'm not moving on like I should be. That I am not living my life."

Her eyes were hooded, and her cheeks bloomed a light shade of pink while gently laying her menu on the table.

"I considered canceling, but I felt bad leaving all alone tonight, and she insisted I go." Natalia slid her hands to the glass in front of her. Her eyes were now fixated on the clear object. Cupping it, she began wiping the perspiration from it.

"Well then, I think she's one of my new best friends."

The light tone of Nick's voice had Natalia's head lifting. Natalia's mouth spread in a smile when their eyes locked.

"Even if you don't see this going anywhere, at least you got out and had a good dinner."

Beaming a smile back, Nick was rewarded with a sexy chuckle that had her skin prickling with goosebumps. She tried to ignore her body's reaction and failed miserably.

"We will see about the good dinner thing… I can be very picky." She winked.

Her body was caving to the need to reach across the table and make physical contact, but before she allowed the urge to take control, she looked around the restaurant floor. Scanning the room filled with couples and families, she noted a waiter shifting between a few tables.

He was cheerful and relaxed, making small talk with other patrons. Natalia's inaudible sweet voice was in the background of noise as Nick watched him make his way over to their table. The warmth of his smile was inviting. With the fluid motion of someone who had done it many times, he pulled out a notepad and pen from his apron.

Looking him over, Nick assumed he couldn't have been no older than twenty. The tall, lanky frame and pasty appearance had her wondering if he got out in the sun very much.

"Well, hey, Nick!" A voice boomed from across the room.

Hearing her name called out, she turned to see a familiar face coming to stand next to the confused waiter. The young man paused, pen in hand, to watch the interaction.

"Oh, hey Ricky! How are you?"

"Good," He responded. His hand shot out. The firm grip warm when she shook in greeting.

"I haven't seen you around here in weeks. Been hiding from us, I guess."

"I have been busy with my most recent client," nodding her head to the woman across the table. "This is Natalia. She's moving into town."

Ricky smiled and nodded at Natalia. "Welcome. I am sure you will love it here."

Natalia's face tinted a darker shade of pink as she nodded her head in response. Nick grinned bigger, her back sitting a bit straighter, and took both their menus.

Noting the waiter frowning at the table in impatience, Nick handed them over. The young man took them, tucking them under his arm with a smile.

"We'll both have the special. An ice tea for me and ..." Pausing for Natalia to answer.

Timidly she responded, "A Sprite for me, thanks."

"Perfect. I will get these put in right away."

"Get these beautiful women whatever they need, Mike."

Ricky's comment had Natalia turn a lush red color. Nick was getting concerned that she might pass out from embarrassment.

Clearing his throat, Ricky patted the boy on the shoulder. The young man, still standing patiently next to him, nodded. Without a word, he winked and walked away.

"Good. Well, ladies," He said, turning back to face them, "I have to get moving. Enjoy your meal." Nodding, he patted the table and left to mingle with others as he went.

"Do you always order like that for people? Or am I just special? I've never let anyone else order for me, which was kind of strange."

Nick was surprised to hear the tiniest bit of annoyance in her voice. Maybe she wasn't as embarrassed as she thought.

"I figured you would like to try something that is new and different." Placing her elbows on the table and leaning forward. "Ricky is the manager. I know it will be good." When Natalia opened her mouth to speak, she pushed on to add, "And no, I'm not gonna tell you what it is. It's going to be a surprise."

Snapping her mouth shut caused her teeth to click. Although frowning, the wrinkles marring her forehead resolved. Natalia sat back in her seat, her eyes scanning the room around them.

The pause in conversation allowed her to observe the view in front of her. The pallet of Natalia's body was alluring. Drinking in every curve made her mind wander. Lowering over the lines of her neck and resting atop her supple cleavage, her eyes craved more.

What I wouldn't give to lick my way....

The mental image her mind created ignited a fire inside her. Shifting in her seat, she appreciated that no one else could read her mind. Needing to think about something else before she was a puddle on this chair, she swallowed down the desire and tried to make small talk.

"So, tell me about you."

Green round eyes landed back on hers. A dim light shined in them, pulling Nick in further. Long eyelashes fluttered, and her hushed "Oh?" caused something to stir inside her.

Nick's voice lowered in octave, "I want to know all the good, bad, and mysterious things about Natalia Purez."

༄

With the sensual tone, Natalia felt herself melting between her legs. Talking helped push past the sexual tension. In the beginning, she attributed the few awkward moments to her embarrassment about talking about personal things. Attempting to be upfront about her past relationship problems gave her more anxiety, but she figured if she were going to go through with this dinner, she would heed Rachel's advice and not hold anything back.

Nick deserved to know the truth about Dan. The woman across from her listened intently, taking in all the information that was given without judgment or prejudice. The anxiety of explaining every detail oozed out of her like blood after getting cut by a scalpel.

An odd sense of freedom came with unloading to someone she barely knew. The sensation is equivalent to a therapy session and getting a deep tissue massage simultaneously.

This interaction went on for a long time. She couldn't remember the last time she had sat down and talked about herself like this. Typically, she pushed personal affairs aside and discussed business or medical advancements. Their plates had been emptied, and the dessert menu was brought out before long.

"That was amazing." She replied, rubbing the small food baby and pushing against her zipper. "What exactly was it I was filling my mouth with?"

Handing over the empty plate to Nick, she stacked them in the middle of the table. Their hands brushed, and she tried holding back another blush but failed.

"It was four-cheese ravioli. They use a special seasoning in the cheese as well as the sauce. I had a hunch you'd like it."

Lacing her fingers together, Nick leaned toward her. The smell of her perfume invited Natalia also to lean forward.

"So, do you know what you want for dessert?" Nick asked.

Oh, you have no idea.

Internally, she smiled at herself as naughty ideas filled her mind. Opening her mouth, Nick shifted, halting her words, picked up the dessert menu, and handed it over to her. Cautiously, she took it, and their hands brushed again.

This time she knew it was on purpose. Nick's fingers lingered a bit too long before pulling away, and she reveled in the sensations the contact created. This woman had so much to offer her, and so far, she hasn't found one thing she dislikes.

"I think I'm just going to get a vanilla malt." Her tongue slid over her bottom lip. "Anything bigger than that, and I don't think I'll make it home." Fire danced behind her eyes as hormones raged inside of her. "What are you going to have?"

"I think I'm gonna have the same thing. It sounds like a good choice." She said with a hitch to her voice.

After dessert was ordered, Nick excused herself to go to the restroom, giving Natalia time to take a few breaths and collect herself. The food was delivered as Nick reappeared. Natalia watched the soft pink tongue lazily lick her top lip.

Her eyes eagerly took in the cup in front of her. An image flashed of Nick licking the frozen treat off her sent her heart racing, and she found it hard to retain her breath for a moment. Shaking her head, she picked up her glass and took a big gulp of cool liquid through her straw. Unable to still the carnival of scenes her mind still conjured up.

"So, tell me why you didn't want to go through with this dinner?" Nick inquired, "Is it just your past with Dan that was holding you back or something else?"

Reaching across the table, Nick picked up her hand and examined it. Her mind was telling her to answer that air released from her lungs forcefully, moving the napkin on the table.

I hope you can handle the truth.

Squeezing her strong hand, she replied, "It was a few things." *Here we go.* "I don't think I could start something else without truly being over Dan. It wouldn't be fair to the other person to keep dragging that backup."

Natalia slid her hand from Nick's, resting back against her seat. The corners of her mouth dipped, and a hollow feeling filled her chest.

"Plus, it doesn't seem right when I am a client. I do believe in keeping my professional life separate from my personal one."

The frown on Nick's face had a sour sensation twisting in her gut. She didn't like the feeling and moved a bit to try to starve it off, making it worse.

"And I guess just the thought of starting over from the beginning... with someone... well, it's scary for me." She admitted. "I'm not used to the dating part anymore."

Nick noticed the way she had run her hands over her face. The way she studied her in silence made her self-conscious, and when she leaned further forward and stretched out her hand again, Natalia had an odd calm wash over her.

Pausing, she bit her lip, fighting an internal monologue until giving in. Placing her hand back in Nick's sturdy ones, she followed the other woman's eyes as they fell to her mouth. The suggestive look had Natalia squeezing her thighs together.

"So...."

Nick blinked a few times, lifting her eyes back to her face. The stroking of her thumb over the back of her knuckles was soothing and sensual, and Natalia never wanted to let go.

"I can understand how you're feeling." The consistent stroking calmed her racing heart. "Although if you are in a relationship with someone, they are going to need to know about your past. It is a part of you."

"You're right," she commented.

"You can't hide from it." Nick continued. "We all have a past. To love another person, to want to be with them, means accepting everything about them."

"Yes-"

"Things happen in life, and those things brought us together." The circles stopped, and Natalia looked down at their joined fingers as Nick gently squeezed.

"So why not just see where it goes? If something is uncomfortable or scary to you, just let me know."

Nick's voice dropped, and her next words came out in a low whisper that Natalia needed to watch her mouth as she spoke.

"At least give me a chance."

Natalia's heart clenched in her chest at the soft plea.

Rising from her seat, never letting go of her hand, Nick made her way around the table to her. Natalia's heart pounded into her rib cage at the look in Nick's eyes. Her mouth tilted up at the corner.

"How about a dance?"

"We haven't finished our dessert yet." Waving her free hand towards the glasses sitting on the table.

"I'm not so hungry anymore. Besides… if you want, I'll order you another before we leave."

"You don't have to do that."

Laying money down on the table, Nick gently pulled Natalia to her feet. A slow song started as they stepped onto the crowded dance floor. Pulling her against the heat of her chest, Nick wrapped her arms tightly around her waist. A tingling had her tensing at first but only lasted a second.

A stir of reassurance engulfed her. All Natalia's senses were on full alert and accelerated the longer they embraced. Nick's hands running up and down her back and their thighs rubbing against one another caused her involuntarily panting.

Her chest constricted, and she became breathless at the swell of Nick's breast pressing against hers, mingling with the smell of their perfumes. The smell amplified when Natalia laid her head on Nick's shoulder and inhaled the scent of her lavender shampoo.

The pressure of Nick's hand rubbing up and down her back in a fluid caress made her nipples rock hard. The tight peaks moved against her bra, and the friction sent shocks all the way from her torso down to settle between her thighs. The prickling made her soak her underwear.

Natalia knew Nick noticed when the arm around her, tugged her even more tightly. Electricity radiated between them. Lifting her head, Nick's eyes dropped to her lips. The alluring movement of her throat as she swallowed tempted her to trail her tongue down her skin.

The energy around them intensified. Desire filled Nick's eyes, making a silent wish. They clouded over in a trance. Keeping herself from giving in to the urge to tear Nick's clothes off on this wooden dance floor became increasingly challenging. Reinforcing Natalia's need to leave every second.

Without notice, Nick grabbed her hand. Pulling her out the front door. Nick's pace increases with every step towards Natalia's car. The air rushed out of her when Nick gripped her upper arms and maneuvered their bodies so her back pressed against the car door.

Wet lips crashed down, claiming hers in a fever. A moan stuck in her throat. Clinging to Nick as if she needed her to breathe. The rational part of her brain was telling her to slow down, but her hands had overruled her mind. Chills ran down her spine at the nudging of her tongue. Parting her lips, Nick greedily entered her mouth, instantly making her wet.

Natalia's body took over, pushing her thigh between Nick's legs, and she was happily greeted by the heat she felt there. Moaning, she started rocking against Nick's sex. A sweet satisfaction played through her at Nick's guttural moan into her mouth as she plunged her tongue deep, seeking more.

Signals went off like sirens in Natalia's head when warm fingers slid under her shirt. Pulling her hands out, Natalia pushed Nick's lower body away, breaking their kiss and forcing her to back up.

"I'm so sorry. I didn't hurt you, did I?"

The flush of Nick's face counteracted the deep lines creasing her forehead. Brushing her clothes off, Nick took another step backward. Straightening her clothes, Natalia attempted some more space by edging down the side of the door.

"It's okay," standing at attention, trying to collect herself, "I just can't do this right here right now."

A few more deep breaths helped clear some of the fog in her mind. "I need some time. I hope you understand."

"Of course."

A peculiar feeling filled the air around them. She would have found the atmosphere amusing if it didn't remind her of the weather right before a storm.

"I should let you get going. It's getting late." Nick said. The tone of her voice off.

Why can't I just be normal?

Unable to bring herself to look the other woman in the eyes, fearing Nick might feel guilty if she saw her upset. Instead, she folded her arms over her chest, trying to keep herself from reaching out.

"I have an early morning also." Mumbling through the knot forming in her throat, Natalia lifted her eyes enough to see Nick place her hands in her pockets.

"I'll see you in a few days for the inspections?"

"Of course."

Natalia lifted her eyes at Nick's approach. Placing a light kiss on her lips, she added, "I had a great time tonight. Drive safe."

Batting her eyes hid the tornado of emotions behind her placid eyes. Natalia wondered when she would reach the eye of the storm to grant her a pause and ability to think.

"Me too. It was amazing."

Natalia's smile did not quite reach her eyes. Even though she wasn't cold, she rubbed her arms against the chill she felt in her bones.

"You make sure you get home all right."

Waving, she watched Nick walk across the gravel parking lot and get into her car. Standing there, watching Nick drive off, she had to collect herself before getting into her car. Putting the car in reverse, she tried to sort out her confusion over her reactions; all the while, her skin still hummed with need.

Chapter 19

"It just goes to show, that you don't even have to be here to tease me. I mean, my goodness, it's been two days, and you're still not going to let up, are you?"

Coming back from dinner the other night, walking softly up the staircase, and gingerly opening her door, she hoped to be alone with her thoughts. Expecting Rachel to be in bed fast asleep, allowing her an uninterrupted shower to collect herself and fall into bed, but she was disturbed the moment the door swung open.

Walking in, Rachel bombarded her with questions and wouldn't leave her alone until answering all of them to her friend's curious satisfaction. Remembering the interrogation had her rolling her eyes and her mind getting tired all over again.

Dropping her friend off at the airport, Natalia was under the assumption that she would be able to get away from the constant teasing.

Oh, how wrong I was.

"Hey! I'm just glad you found someone that is willing to tame you." A teasing giggle filled the air, "I mean, that woman is gonna need all the luck in the world to handle you."

Laughing at her joke, had Natalia sporting a half-smile. A small snort sounded, and both women were in hysterics.

"Did you just snort?" Her giggling calmed down after a moment.

"I was just remembering the look on your face…" Another snort came over the line. "When you walked in the door was priceless."

Rachel paused to catch her breath. A wheezing cough rang in her ear, causing Natalia to pull the phone away from her ear till it ceased. Her friend already continuing when she rested the receiver back against her ear. "… like a five-year-old with a shiny new toy. From what I heard, it sounded like you *enjoyed* your time with her."

"Okay. Okay." The humor of the moment edging. "Could we talk about something else, please? I'm really starting to regret telling you what happened."

Even though she knew her friend was just playing at giving her a hard time, Natalia still didn't enjoy it. It was becoming more annoying by the second.

"Fine then." The laughter died as she steered the conversation away from that night. "How did your inspections go?"

"They- "

"The place isn't going to fall down, is it?"

"No, it- "

"Was Nick there with you?"

Thankful for the slight subject change, Natalia eased back into her seat.

"No, it's not going to fall down," She assured her. "I'm on my way back to the bed and breakfast now. It didn't even take that long."

Pausing, she flicked on her car blinker and looked in her mirrors. Resuming the conversation after she turned.

"The problems they told me about were minor."

The nonchalant tone did not quite match the growing impatience she was feeling.

"Like the appliances needed to be updated, the roof needs to be replaced within five years, some old termite damage in the barn, and the windows need replacing."

A mental checklist flashed in her mind with a timeline to complete it. Wind softly blew pollen against her windshield, reminding her of the changing seasons and only adding to her checklist of things to get done.

"It is a house, after all. You couldn't expect it to be in brand new condition."

Knowing all too well that her friend rolled her eyes as she spoke, Natalia lifted the corner of her mouth. "Granted, it may cost some money, but it could have been a lot worse."

The crack of her back and shoulder as she pried herself out of the driver's seat had her groaning. Giving her body a much-needed stretch felt amazing. Sore muscles protested at the tension from a long day of driving.

"Well, it sounds like you got a good deal, and that house is stunning."

Chewing sounds crinkled over the line. A low rumble reminded Natalia that she hadn't eaten all morning. Another groan slipped as she regretted not stopping for a bite earlier.

"There was no electrical or plumbing to be done?" Muffled by a mouthful of something. "You know you still never answered my other question. Trying to dodge it? Hmm…?"

Wow, she's persistent.

Usually, that would be a quality Natalia would encourage from her friend, but for some reason, today, it was irritating, possibly because it was directed at her instead of an unsuspecting client. Natalia waited to answer. Slowly she made her way up the front porch. Her bones creaked along with the steps as she made her way towards the inviting rocking chairs and sat down.

"No, I'm not trying to dodge anything." Her jaw clenched, and she mentally had to relax. "She was there and only stayed just long enough for the inspection."

The rocking from the chair had her eyes growing heavy. The soft, tender movements drawing her into a sweet calm. Her words came out drawn and thick.

"She said she had another inspection to be at," A Yawn escaped her lips. "And told me she would call me later. So that's what I expect she is going to do. Satisfied?"

Drifting her eyes closed, Natalia listened to the sounds around her. Crickets chirped in unison with the cicadas. Sun warmed her shoes with a gentle kiss.

"Cool your feathers and retract your claws," Rachel replied defensively. "I was just trying to see if anything happened. You're getting so defensive lately." Her sarcasm mixed with regret, "What's wrong?".

With a sigh, Natalia opened her eyes. Unsure how to answer, she took in the white-washed ceiling above her. The lines and groves stole her focus and distracted her long enough that Rachel cleared her throat. The sound echoed into her ear and pulled her back to the question she asked.

"It's nothing," she replied. "I just don't like talking about this." She imagined her friend frowning and rolling her eyes at her. "I mean, it's all new to me, and I'm not used to being on the *prowl* anymore."

Her admission did not phase Rachel. With a chuckle, she bluntly responded with,

"Prowl."

Natalia's mouth quirked up at the corner, even as her eyebrows furrowed together. *She is relentless*, she thought, shaking her head.

"Ummmm, no." Her tone light but serious. "Please... unless I bring it up, can we just talk about normal things?"

"I can do that," Rachel said, "We'll just talk about normal boring things from now on," agreeing for the sake of the conversation. "But, not right now." Noting the shift in discussion. "I got called into work a day early *because* one of the other techs quit.... again."

The annoyance in her voice was not lost on her. Worried swirled around in the pit of Natalia's stomach, but the reality is it isn't her concern anymore.

"They are shorthanded," She sighed. "So, I gotta run. I'll call you later and fill you in, okay?"

"Okay. Talk to you later."

The solid wood of the rocking chair rested against the back of her head. Her eyes fluttered shut and she turned to rest her cheek against the warm surface.

The wind rustling the branches on the willows and the grass whistling against the breeze offered her a sense of contentment. A feeling she longed for. Being saturated with the memories of the past lately had an aftertaste of confusion-tinged pain.

After their dinner a few nights ago, the awkward and uncomfortable emotions started to fade away. The nerves and anxiety didn't start the moment she opened her eyes, and it gave her a reprieve of peace. Now, Natalia was beginning to understand what it meant just to let things go and move on.

The descending sun upon her face and the familiar sense of drifting off quieting her being was interrupted when she heard her name being called in the distance. Inwardly groaning, she cracked open one eye to see a swollen figure approaching. Natalia jumped up, rubbing at her eyes.

I must be dreaming. Right?

The figure approached, pulling a suitcase behind.

Dan?

∽

How could this be happening?

Blinking, she tried to focus on the person before her. With wide open eyes, her brain tried to make excuses for what she was seeing.

No. No. No.

At first, she thought she was daydreaming.

Not now! This is not happening!

Shaking her head, noticing Dan still moving closer, proved that it was a daydream. Her racing heart competed with the dismal gnawing in her chest. After all this time, when she was finally starting to return to a normal existence, this person had to stir things up again.

Her body took over, and Natalia shot up from the rocking chair. The porch tilted, dizzy from standing too fast, forcing her body to collapse back down into the rocking chair. Dan's head snapped up. Observing her fall, the other woman ran up the steps.

"Are you okay? Nothings hurt, right?"

Hovering next to her, with brows drawn together, she asked again if Natalia was ok. Gently, Dan rested the back of her hand against her forehead while rubbing her upper arm.

The contact of Dan's skin touching her made her skin coil back. Involuntarily her body jerked away. An odd sensation filled her. A couple of months ago, Natalia would have given anything for Dan to hold her and just tell her it would all be okay. Looking back on it now, the lie would have only delayed the inevitable.

Dan's unwelcome arms wrapping around her shoulders brought reality crashing back down upon her. Frustration and repulsion boiled up and exploded as she pushed her away. Folding her arms, dismissing the other woman's attempt to try again, Natalia stood her ground. Every part of her was screaming to flee, to get away from this creature that broke her, but her mind forced her body to remain still.

I won't give her the satisfaction.

"What are you doing here?" The words hissed out through clenched teeth.

Dan backed up into the railing as if she had been hit. Her eyes gleamed and opened wide.

"How did you find me?!" Natalia demanded. Rage made her bolder than she normally would have been. "This is very inappropriate, Dan. You have no right to be here."

Dan's cheeks burned a bright red, and she dropped her eyes. The attempts to reach for her died in an instant. The other woman was seemingly embarrassed by the fierceness in Natalia's voice.

Looking away, she replied, "I'm sorry. I missed you so much and – and just wanted to see you." Her words soft and pleading. "I found out where you went from some of the girls at your old practice."

"Oh? Really?" *Nice to know.*

"Don't be mad." The pouty lower lip had no effect on her. "I didn't want to leave things unresolved like they were."

Lifting her head, Dan attempted to meet her gaze, but Natalia shifted her eyes away.

"I thought we both owed each other that much."

Natalia let out a half-hearted laugh. The sound of it mimicking her lack luster need to keep this conversation going.

"Rich."

"Come on, Nat." Dan's hand lifted and fell at her statement. "We need to talk."

Another laugh accompanied by a scoff. Natalia rolled her eyes and shook her head.

"It just didn't feel right being away from you."

"You have to be joking." Disdain dripped off the words so thickly it felt like spitting paint.

Turning to walk down the stairs, Dan sighed. She watched her grab her bag and bring it to where she stood on the porch. Disbelief still thrumming through her.

"I don't know what you want from me?" Exasperation poured out, "I don't think you should be here. You made it perfectly clear who you wanted, and I dealt with it."

Taking a step toward her, Natalia put her hand up, effectively halting her. Shaking her head, "Can't you just leave things be?"

Turning, intending to walk away and create some space between them, but Dan grabbed her arm and pulled her back around. The contact made her skin crawl. The sound of her back teeth grinding filled her ears as she fought the urge to smack her hand away.

"I want to talk. Get things out in the open."

Yeah. Sure, she thought.

I'm not running away just because you tell me to." The pitch of her voice rising, "I can wait if that's what it takes, but we will talk."

Clenching her fists, she bit out, "Fine, we'll talk, but not now."

Turning, she looked her straight in the eye. Nothing but disgust and irritation when she added, "Look, I don't know what you're hoping to find by coming here," she breathed heavily through her nose. "But I do know it won't be me. I left all that behind when I left Tennessee, and that's where it is staying. In the past."

Natalia shook off Dan's hand. Spinning back around, she quickly fled inside. Her inner child wanted to stomp her feet as she went but refrained.

Retorting an echo of "Goodnight" over her shoulder when pulling open the front door.

I never want to see you again.

A simple reply of, "See you in the morning," followed the creek of the front door swinging shut behind her.

Let's hope you don't.

Chapter 20

Working nonstop for twelve days was wearing her down, and she wasn't sure how long she could keep going. Showing after showing with endless amounts of paperwork, including a glitch with the MLS system, had her stocking up on migraine medicine.

After dealing with another couple that argued constantly over every small detail, Nick was ready to rip her hair out. The idea of being bald, as unappealing as drinking gasoline, was the only thing preventing her from going through with it.

Finally able to get some much overdue time off, her head ached as she soldiered on. The rain, seemingly wanting to pierce the ground as it fell, still couldn't pull her spirits down.

For days, her thoughts were consumed with a tempting smile and lush skin, leaving her craving more. Eyes that sparkled and lips that made her want to sin first and beg for forgiveness later.

The woman who strode into town only a few weeks ago had stolen the pieces of her heart. The simple yet meaningful interactions they shared had taken up permanent residence in her soul. Her body pulsed with memories, unable to get the visions of Natalia pressed up against her car out of her head.

Providing her with ample wet dreams that had her questioning if she should buy stock in linen from her recent visits to the store to replace her soaked bedsheets. The attraction grew to an infatuation that now affected her focus at work.

Today, her goal was to clear her head by focusing on the settlement of the Olsen's place. Closing this deal is crucial to move on to her next sale.

Sales are a part of my income, she reminded herself. It would also be the first day, in ten days, that she would have talked to Natalia, let alone see her. She needed to devise something fantastic to make up for ignoring her.

A day filled with errands and paperwork was the last thing she wanted to do, but it was a necessary evil. Every single time she was going to call, something else would come up, forcing her to push it off.

Nerves gnawed at her now that she would have to pay the price for being an imbecile and letting her work come first. In the past, this wouldn't bother her. Most of the women she dated understood, but this time it didn't sit right with her.

This one is different, she told herself. This one made her want to try harder.

Changing out of her work clothes and into something more comfortable, Nick made a quick stop by the local florist and picked up a dozen purple tulips. At her request, the florist packed them in a white box. The smell of them was intoxicating.

Next, she headed out of town in search of the perfect gift. The drive past all the local shops gave her a sentimental feeling, putting her in an even better mood. Shops dotted the quaint neighboring town. It didn't take too long to find what she was looking for.

Nick paid, happy with her surprise, and set off for the peaceful drive back.

Figuring food was in order, she pulled up and parked out front of the deli to pick Natalia and her up some lunch. The thrum of a light shower beat down on the hood of her car as she pulled her keys out of the ignition.

Here we go; tucking her chin down, she pulled the hoodie she left in the car over her head and opened her door. Running in, she hunched over, trying to keep as dry as possible. The ring of the bell attached to the door greeted her when she stepped into the friendly surroundings.

The young server gave a warm smile as Nick ordered two ham and cheese sandwiches with all the fixings. While waiting, she took in the room and noticed a familiar figure sitting in one of the back booths. About to go over, Nick stopped when another woman walked up.

Picking up on the intimate way the woman caressed her shoulder before sitting down, Nick got the feeling they closely knew each other. A lump formed in her throat, thick and heavy, at the manner in which the other woman grabbed and held onto her hand and stared into her eyes.

Suddenly, she was glad that it was raining because it was the only time she wore her hoodie. With her face mostly uncovered, she was going unnoticed. She was grateful because what she was witnessing was tugging at her heart in all the wrong ways. It became almost too painful to stand there watching their intimacy.

By the time the food arrived, her hunger had dissipated, and she felt a bit sick to her stomach.

Taking note of the concerned look on the young server's face, she briskly paid and rushed back out to her car. Damp and a slurry of emotions banged on the steering wheel over and over.

I can't believe I thought there was something there. A burning behind her eyes unrelenting to her need to calm down. Mulling in her head, *it's my own fault for not keeping in touch more often.*

The palm of her hand began to hurt the more she struck her steering wheel. Hating the way she handled things and telling herself:

Serves me right! I'm so stupid! Stupid. Stupid. STUPID!

Chiding herself as tears stung at her eyes.

Even frowning, she looked amazing. I just wish I knew what they were talking about.

෴

Emotions swirled around inside her, all battling for attention, as she stood and made her way outside. Shielding her eyes against the setting sun, Natalia ignored the light drizzle.

That was odd, seeing a vehicle screech out of a parking spot onto the road.

"… I realized I'm lost without you."

Dan whined from behind her. The comment only pressed on her already frayed patience. Pausing, Dan leaned over her protruding belly, catching her breath. The rain cleared up as the restaurant door clicked shut.

"I don't feel right anymore!" Dan hollered into the empty space around them. Straightening as much as she could, she pressed a hand against her arching back.

"Being with Rick just wasn't the same. He doesn't- he doesn't make me feel like you do. I think... I want to give us another try."

Spinning around, Natalia almost collided with her. The movement made her vision blur for the briefest of seconds.

"Maybe it will..."

Eyes widened at the woman in front of her. The same woman who made her feel more disconcerted for every second that passed.

"Wait. A. Second."

She made sure to sound out every word pointedly, leaving no room to mistake their intent. Taking two steps closer, Natalia folded her arms over her chest, causing Dan to back up.

"Don't even think for one minute that you can intrude back into my life, say you're sorry, and everything will be okay."

Natalia's hand flew up, stopping the other woman from commenting.

"Let's get one thing straight right now. I don't want to be with you."

Sighing, she ignored the tears streaking down Dan's cheeks.

"This," making a show of pointing between them, "is never going to happen. Never again."

A low cry escaped from the other woman. With her hands on her hips, Natalia ground her back teeth together, trying to contain her growing irritation.

"It has taken me a long time, a *looong* time, to get over what you did and how you treated me." Her words were flat and losing their edge.

"I only agreed to have this conversation because you weren't going to go away until I did. Now, I am regretting it."

Frustration was giving way to exhaustion over having to deal with this particular person still. Her mind wanted a break, and she wished that the person across from her was a sexy realtor who gave her goosebumps in all the right ways.

She missed her. After not hearing from her for several days and only getting her voicemail, it made her think that she might not have felt as deep a connection as she did. Her mind wondered if Nick wasn't interested anymore.

One problem at a time.

Closing her eyes, she pinched the bridge of her nose. Dan, the woman who stepped out on her, stood in front of her, pregnant and crying. Sighing, she blew out a breath and opened her eyes. She would have to deal with the problem in front of her before she could even contemplate what to do about Nick.

"I don't see the point in you even being here."

"I know-"

"I already told you before I don't want to see you anymore."

"Come on, Nat. We can-"

"There is nothing left to talk about."

"But-"

"I'm sorry about how you feel, but you made your bed now you must lie in it."

Another cry escaped Dan's lips, and Natalia frowned.

"The only person who can be blamed for your actions, is you, and if you had any sense of self-preservation left,"

Dan's face flamed.

"You'll get some help before you hurt that baby growing inside of you."

The other woman's cheeks became brighter than a blistering sunburn, and Natalia worried she wasn't breathing.

"How dare you!" She screamed in an irate fury. Words flew from her lips like a swarm of angry wasps. "I can't believe that you said that to me! After I read that letter you sent me, I realized I had made a huge mistake! I really thought we had something, and I didn't just want to let it all go."

Damn, now she's crying again.

Crossing her arms over her chest, Dan stood ridged. Her stance rigid.

"I wanted you to be in my life!"

Gone were the tears and sorrow-filled eyes. She swiped angrily at the last of the wetness. Ice filled her cold stare, and she sniffed back her runny nose.

"I came here to try and own up to everything, but you are impossible! Serves me right for even thinking you had a soul."

A hand ran across her forehead, moving the strand of hair sticking to her damp face.

"Damn hormones," She mumbles. A curse escaped her lips, and she swallowed.

Natalia stood there, silent under the assault of angry slurs and comments. She didn't have the energy to argue back, nor did she even want to. She didn't see the point in it anymore.

"Fine, if you don't want to see me anymore, you won't have to."

Collecting herself, Dan brushed some invisible lint off her top.

"I'll leave you alone."

Handing Natalia a piece of paper, Dan frowned. The sadness no longer masked by her rage at the situation.

"I just want you to have this. It seems that I don't need it anymore."

Watching Dan walk away gave Natalia an odd sensation. She concluded that she should have been sad, but remarkably, she wasn't. Finally, alone, Natalia opened the paper to reveal the photo of Dan and her on their first date.

Accompanied by the picture was the first letter she had sent her. Looking over the worn paper and film felt foreign. Her fingers flipped over the photo, reading the written words on the back that read *'soul mates for life.'*

The familiar curves of her script stared back at her. The memory of writing that and giving it to Dan on their first anniversary came to her in a faraway haze. It all seemed like another person's life now. Grazing her fingertips over the faded colors of the photograph, she tried to feel some sort of attachment. Some sort of sadness at this situation they were now in.

Her inability to even drench up those kinds of emotions towards Dan anymore solidified that she had done the right thing. Placing the photo back into the paper and stuffing it into her back pocket, she inhaled a deep breath. Allowing her lungs to expand and fully release, hoping to relieve some tension.

On to the next problem.

Reigning herself to another long conversation that she was sure wasn't going to be much fun, she made her way back to her car.

$\mathcal{C}$*hapter* 21

Time seemed pleasantly endless on her drive back to the B&B. The languid trip proved to tip things in her favor. Walking in, Gracie informed her that Dan had left. Wrinkles creased her forehead as she mentioned how upset and confused Dan looked.

Gracie also made a point to inform her that Nick came by to drop off something. Shrugging when Natalia arched an eyebrow, the elderly woman told her Nick placed it in her room.

Not expecting that, Gracie smiled at Natalia's obvious surprise. Natalia adored the elderly lady's smile. The endearing crinkles gave a distinguished yet homey vibe. A frown quickly replaced the smile, and before she could ask, Gracie mumbled to herself about having to clean up the kitchen. Guessing what that could be referencing, Natalia followed Gracie as she made her way around the front desk and hurried out of the room.

On the way up to her room, a funny unease gave her goosebumps. Hair raised on her arms, a tell-tale sign that something was amiss. At a loss of an explanation, a headache crept behind her eyes.

The feeling subsided as quickly as it had come after she opened the door and saw two white boxes lying on the bed. Elation filled her at the sight of them. Moving toward the bed, she reached for one of the boxes but froze.

An overwhelming need to shower had her dropping her hand and turning in the direction of the bathroom. Her mind gave her no other option but to wash off the stench from earlier.

Dirty.

That single word did not fully elope the unclean sensation their conversation at lunch left inside her. A soft ambiance surrounded her as the slight mist of the heat from the shower sprayed down from the faucet, helping to ease her mood.

Peeling off her clothes, the sounds of ripping at the forcefulness behind her movements caused her to cringe. Ignoring the unflattering sensations, Natalia jumped under the spritz of the hot shower. The satisfying sting giving her what she needed.

All the metaphorical slime of the day slipped down her body, pooling at her feet before sliding down the drain. The vanilla and lavender scent of the shampoo soothed all of her senses, allowing her mind to clear.

The tension of her muscles gave way, and she slumped against the shower stall, fighting to keep her body upright and her eyes open. Sleep called to her from afar, and she knew fighting it off would be a losing battle.

A knock on the door echoed through her room, reaching through her sleep-deprived state. Turning off the shower, her bones cracked, and her body lagged as she stepped out. Remembering to pull on a robe, she took the few steps to get to the door.

What now? I am exhausted.

The door swung open with a creek and she was greeted with a smiling Gracie standing on the other side, holding a steaming bowl of soup. The drawn-out gurgle of her stomach brought heat to her face. The tiredness of her mind argued with the hunger of her empty stomach.

"You didn't have to do that. I would have come down if I got hungry."

"If?" Gracie quipped. A knowing lift to the corner of her mouth as she held out the bowl.

Giving in, Natalia took the hot bowl. The aroma of the hearty potato soup was so alluring that her mouth instantly watered.

"I'm going to go out with the girls this evening." Gracie motioned towards the warm bowl. "I won't be able to scrounge up some food later."

The steam wafted up, and she got another whiff of the delicious smells. A rumble sounded louder.

"I thought I'd bring you a little something so you don't go hungry.

Natalia couldn't protest after her stomach growled in response. Gracie chuckled and nodded.

"Now, go eat, and I'll see you in the morning."

Patting her arm, the elderly woman turned and headed down the stairs.

"Make sure you finish it all." She yelled over her shoulder.

"She must be a mind reader." Mumbling to herself as she closed the door. Her nose lowered to the bowl, and she breathed in the aroma again. "This is exactly what I needed."

As she ate, she pondered what could be in the boxes. Anticipation consumed her as she imagined everything from a bat to an engagement ring, although she highly doubted the last one. Taking her time to drain her bowl, Natalia procrastinated further by getting into pajamas.

Those boxes sat there, tempting her to open them, and now fully cleaned, fed, and clothed, she no longer had an excuse. Rolling her neck, soft pops filling the room, she pushed back her nervous excitement and picked up the larger of the two boxes.

Upon opening the first box, a strong scent of tulips greeted her. It collided with her nose in a sweet and sensual way, like a silk ribbon wrapping around her body. Not wanting to disturb the flowers from their resting place, Natalia gingerly removed the card. The words were not registering, so she had to re-read the note a couple of times.

I'm so sorry for not keeping in touch. I've been so busy. I hope this shows that I'm not planning on going away unless you want me to. I'm not afraid of a little competition, but if you want to remain just friends, please tell me.

What is she talking about?

Natalia didn't understand. Her brows drew together in contingent thought while her mind raced with many different questions. She didn't want Nick to go away.

Didn't I make that clear at dinner? Did something change?

Not liking this limbo, Natalia got a pressing urge to talk to Nick. Reaching for her keys, she realized she didn't know where Nick lived. The weight of the keys heavy in her palm as her stomach decided if it wanted to do flip flops or tie itself up in knots. Calling her wasn't satisfying, and she wanted to see her face when they spoke.

The house settlement was tomorrow. She would have to wait and see her then. Sighing, tomorrow couldn't come soon enough, but she would make it very clear she wanted Nick in her life. Validating her own feelings, she would confirm that Nick isn't the only one who wants this relationship to continue.

$\mathcal{C}$hapter 22

Today is going to be a long day.

The inability to shut her mind off the night before had her incapable of concentrating. Drowsiness blanketed her, along with the compelling need to go and straighten things out with Nick. Weighting heavily on her conscious, her mind spun scenarios consistently throughout the night that leaked into the day.

Pacing around her room while getting dressed became more of a chore than a necessity. This impotence of controlling her thoughts left her unable even to enjoy picking out her clothes, which was flustering. Her scattered mind similar to a ball of yarn mixed with too many different colors. Only focusing on one string, she needed to untangle the rest to get to the one she sought, Nick.

Wasting time before going downstairs to eat breakfast helped to distract her for the briefest of moments. The walk around her room once again had gone unnoticed. In a distracted haze, she made her bed and picked up her clothes.

The simple task helped to calm her down long enough to allow other messages into her head. An invisible lightbulb went off in her brain, reminding her there was another box next to the flowers on the bed from the night before. Lightly chewing at her fingernails, she tried remembering where she had placed it. The simple task irked her.

It wasn't on the bed, the dresser, the nightstand, and nor was it in the chair. Frustration grew, and Natalia crouched down on the floor, looking at other angles. It was there that she spotted the white box underneath the bed. Sitting there as if to say, 'I've been waiting.'

A silence swirled around her until she heard the pulse of her blood in her ears. Picking the package up, she slowly sank onto the mattress. Running her fingers lightly across the surface of the box as if she held a combustible secret. Holding her breath, her fingers worked to open the box. Inside was a gold weeping willow pendant on a box chain.

Five branches had leaves, and on the end of each branch hung tiny gold hoops. Carved in the center of the tree trunk was the caduceus symbol. Turning the pendant over, Natalia saw a single word engraved, "**Hope**."

Forgetting to breathe made her chest hurt and the room spin. Her lungs burned as they finally expanded, taking in a deep gulp of air, allowing her mind to function enough so she could finally form words.

"I never knew someone could be so thoughtful."

A single tear escaped, running down the side of her face as she placed the pendant in its final resting place around her neck. The coolness of the gold was welcome against her heated skin.

Looking back at herself in the mirror, she had a new sensation of confidence and excitement. The tips of her fingers fiddled with the pendant, outlining each branch like she was painting the image into her mind.

Sighing, she picked up her bag. With her mind made up, she squared her shoulders and made one more mental checklist as she scanned the room around her. She was going to settle things with Nick today.

❧

Sitting down to breakfast with Gracie was nice. Famished, she cleared her first plate with no problem. Her second plate wasn't as full, but she dug in as Gracie filled her in on some local gossip.

Listening to her talk about her problems took Nick's mind off of her own.

If only it would last all day, but nonetheless, Gracie got up to remove their plates after she cleared off the last of her food. Normally, Nick would have joked around during her stories of how the guests packed so much that their bags popped open upon entering the B&B, but today she couldn't keep her mind from straying.

Leaning forward, staring at her mouth, attempting to listen intently, couldn't keep her thoughts from wandering back to the images of the previous day. The two women etched into the back of her mind so vividly that she could still smell the sandwiches she threw away.

Something shiny in the far corner of the room caught her eye. Turing, she saw Natalia standing near the buffet talking to Gracie. Both women laughing and smiling, but Natalia's body movement was stiff. Shifting, Natalia's eyes locked on hers from across the room, drawing Natalia's eyebrows together.

Nodding at the same time, Natalia turned back toward Gracie. Leaning toward the elderly woman, she said something before swiveling around and walking over toward her table.

Coming closer, Nick noticed in her distant appearance. The glazed look had her mouth going dry. An unfocused study with dark ridges acknowledged her as she drew near. Nick stood, extending her hand.

Disregarding her outstretched hand, it threw her a bit when warm arms wrapped around her. As the embrace tightened, Nick instinctively buried her nose against her neck, very aware of their bodies pressing together.

A sense of disappointment filled her when their embrace was broken, and she craved to reach for her again. Nick shuddered, and Natalia's face twisted with concern. Her hand slid up Nick's arm and began rubbing. Firm strokes sent delicious shivers throughout her body.

"Are you feeling alright?" Her words soft and reassuring. "Do you need me to get anything?"

"No, no, I'm fine. Just a little cold, but I'll be ok."

She hated how wrong it felt to back away from her touch, but it needed to be done if Nick was going to keep a clear head today. Reigning in her feelings was at the forefront of her mind; however, as Natalia kept her demeanor calm and preserved, the urge to do the same was proving to be difficult.

Natalia's mouth parted, and before she could speak or protest, Nick cut her off.

"We should get going. You don't want to be late for settlement."

Pushing in her chair, Nick glided past Natalia. A hushed comment filled with annoyance came across as a curse.

"We wouldn't want to do that."

No acknowledgment was shown. Having to control her emotions until they could speak in private, caused her to come off as cold and unattached.

I wonder if she received the gifts I left?

Stiffly, Nick crossed the room. No mention or comment followed her as she went. Neglecting to look over her shoulder as she made her way around tables. Gracie's wave confirmed that Natalia was trailing behind her. She acknowledged the gesture with a nod as they filtered out of the door, making their way to her office.

The settlement went incredibly smoothly. All the papers were signed without complications, only taking short of two hours to finalize. Natalia walked out of the office, keys in hand and a few new friends.

In her new elated state, Natalia invited the Olsen's to her neighborhood housewarming party. Sitting at the long conference table, not wanting to intrude on the conversation, Nick overheard her mention it would be in two weeks. The siblings agreed that they would try to attend.

Outside, the wind blew against the windows with an eerie howl mimicking a dog. Nick took in the way Natalia, while still a bit straight in her demeanor, leaned to the side as she laughed with the Olsen's. Surprised to see Natalia pull the pendant she gifted her from below her shirt and rub it between her pointer and thumb.

Shut up, she told the hope building inside her.

All morning, she half wanted to get her alone to talk about yesterday but the other half of her wanted to give her space.

Maybe they are just friends, she reasoned with herself. Different excuses and options bounced around in her head. *Or maybe I took too long and she moved on already.* Thoughts battled inside her, and she wanted them to stop for fear she might go mad.

Instead of confronting her thoughts, worried she might not like the answers she received, she remained stoic during their time together. When the Olsen's murmured their need to be elsewhere, everyone said their goodbye's. Nick watched as the siblings piled into their car, started it, and pulled away, leaving both women alone outside her office doors.

"They are wonderful," Natalia said.

Nick acknowledged her words of praise with a nod. Tilting her head to the side, she smiled out at the almost barren parking lot.

"They are." Nick turned to face her. "Congratulations on the new house, and welcome to town officially."

"Thanks."

The lackluster reply was not lost on her. Falling back on her typical realtor skills, Nick extended her hand, noticeably putting space between them. With a smile that didn't fully reach her eyes, Natalia gripped her hand.

"I hope you love it here as much as I do." Genuinely shaking her hand before releasing.

"I already – "

"Well, I have another appointment to be at in about ten minutes. Let me know if you need anything in regards to moving in."

Pulling her keys out of her pocket, Nick made a show of jingling them in her hand before saying her goodbyes and making her way to her own car. Pulling away, she glanced in her rearview mirror, watching Natalia still standing in front of her office with a frown on her face, chewing her lip, and stroking the pendant between her fingers.

Chapter 23

The last two weeks moved at a snail's pace. Even though things have been buzzing around her, Natalia couldn't seem to get Nick out of her mind. The other woman invaded her thoughts constantly.

Any tasks like brushing her teeth, buying new furniture, updating the roof, grocery shopping, and driving around town became so difficult to do because visions of Nick played in her mind like a carousel. Gas was getting expensive from excessively driving from consistently missing turns.

Tasks had her forcibly busy the day before her housewarming. Running around in circles as if she were a chicken with its head cut off helped relax her continuous memory train. The need for distractions and the constant anxiety understandably made her sluggish at times.

Excited, Rachel couldn't wait another day to see how the new house was progressing. At the mention of having something to talk to her about, Natalia attempted to pry information out of her on the phone, but it proved to be fruitless. Conceding on the subject when her friend held steadfast on telling her in person.

A dry breeze swept across her cheek as she set up furniture on the front porch. A noise catching her attention, she peered through the glinting sun to see a dark blue Dodge Durango rolling down her driveway.

Haphazardly laying down the last tablecloth, Natalia brushed her hands off on her slacks to go greet her friend.

"Wow, the house looks great, Nat!"

A high-pitched explanation rang out as her friend exited the car.

"I can't believe you did it!" she exclaimed gleefully. "You're officially a local."

Grunting, Rachel pulled her luggage out of the backseat and rushed to give her longtime friend a hug.

"I can't wait for all the food I'm gonna chow down on tomorrow. Heck, I'm starving now."

"Okay, okay." Natalia giggled, "You can have some food after you get your things put away," she said in a mock authoritative voice.

Rachel sighed. Pulling her suitcase next to her, she saluted. "Aye, aye, captain."

Natalia giggled again. "Alright," swinging her arm over her friend's shoulder. "Let's get you settled."

While Rachel was getting acquainted with the guest room, Natalia threw together some sandwiches and brought them out onto the porch. A few minutes later, Rachel joined her. Silence – pleasant at first – grew awkwardly, filling the space as her friend sat down to eat.

"So… you said you had something to talk to me about?" The question breaking the uncomfortable quietude. "What's going on?"

Cutting right to the point, unwilling to hold back the eager anticipation building inside her. Rachel took her time to chew and swallow the bite she had taken. The passing moments gnawing at Natalia's impatience.

"Well," swallowing again before wiping at her mouth, "as you know, I haven't been feeling right about being back in Tennessee."

"OK…" She edged, willing the topic to move along.

"I don't have anything there worth waiting around for," Taking another bite of her sandwich. "At least not relationship-wise, and I feel like I need some new scenery." Her words were a bit obscured with her mouth full of food.

"So… what are you saying then?" Shifting in her seat to fully face her, "Nothing wrong, is it?"

Shaking her head, she swallowed down the food.

"Nothing's wrong."

Thank goodness.

"In fact,"

Get on with it…

"Things are starting to get better."

Natalia's eyebrows lifted in surprise. Not holding herself back, Rachel's face beamed as she continued.

"I sold my house back in Tennessee."

"What?!"

"…and I am thinking about buying a place down here."

"Whoa! Hold on a sec."

Mouth falling open, Natalia sat there stunned, while Rachel squealed in delight.

"You did what?! Are you kidding?"

Rachel shook her head. A strand of hair cradled her face.

"That's a big move, Rachel, and out of the blue. Are you sure this is what you want?"

"I'm sure," she replied. Her sandwich clasped in her hand while she happily bobbed her head. Hair whipping around and glinting in the sunlight.

"I've been talking a lot to Evelyn and we decided to go to the next step."

Silence. Stunned silence. Wide-eyed, she stared at her friend. Any more surprises and she might need to take an aspirin.

"I really like her, Nat, and living so far apart isn't working for me anymore."

With sympathetic understanding, Natalia smiled at her.

"Besides, I hate being alone and lonely all the time."

Being able to relate to the situation, Natalia nodded, as her personal situation was a mess.

Wasn't it?

"I'm a big girl, and it's time I start settling down with someone who actually wants to."

"It sounds like you made up your mind."

Rachel smiled brightly. Her cheeks glowed, displaying fine lines at the corners of her eyes.

"At least you're sure about it."

"Yes, Ma'am, I am."

"Good."

"But… I do need a place to stay while I find a house out here." Rachel's eyes fall to her sandwich coyly. "That is if you don't mind a roommate for a little while." Lifting her eyes, she tried giving her best puppy dog eyes, making Natalia laugh.

"I'm sorry. I don't mean to laugh," her comment in response to the harsh frown lines her friend bestowed.

Lifting a hand, she covered her mouth, continuing to giggle. Water filled her eyes by the time she finally got herself under control and dropped her hand to her lap.

"Of course, you can stay here. You think I have a guest room to let my visitors stay in a hotel?"

The frown was once again replaced with a stunning smile.

"Just don't eat all the food, and I want hot water in the morning, young lady."

Dramatically rolling her eyes in a wide arch, Natalia expected to see inside her head.

"Deal," she said, taking a bite of her sandwich. Food muffled her speech, "So, how have things been going with you?"

Chewing, Rachel watched as Natalia's expression shifted from happiness to sorrow. Unable to control her mood.

"Oh, honey," her friend cooed.

Natalia looked away from her. She didn't want or need the pity. Standing, she went to lean against the wood railing.

"It has been hard trying not to think of her every second of every day."

Another light breeze swept her face. The wind helped to keep her tears at bay.

"I have never felt this way. Ever." Closing her eyes on a sigh. "Yet I don't know what to do about it."

"Have you talked to her?"

"I've called her office several times, but her receptionist always says she is out or busy."

Groaning, she looked out over her new front lawn. The scenery was beautiful, but this topic always brought her mood down.

"What am I supposed to do?" Natalia leaned forward, cupping her face in her palms. "I'm just trying to understand and get on with my life."

Pausing at the creaking of the chair behind her. "So, I'm doing alright, considering."

Rachel had gotten up, moving to stand next to her. Rubbing her arm, "I'm so sorry. Maybe …"

"No, don't." Biting the words out. "I don't want to hear any false excuses," she snapped.

Hands falling from her face to grip the railing, she let out a long, tense sigh. Too many mixed emotions roiling inside her.

"I want to hear from her what went wrong."

The smack of the railing echoed. Ignoring the stinging of her hand.

"Why won't she talk to me?!"

Natalia swiveled to face the house. Rachel studied her face with rising concern. Natalia figured her friend could tell she had wiped away tears.

"I'm gonna finish cleaning up for the party tomorrow." Announcing with her solemn tone.

"If you need me, I'll be around."

The reflection of remorse in her friend's eyes had an ache forming in her chest. She hated how pitiful she sounded when she should be happy and excited for tomorrow's events. She had done it. Moved on and started over.

I don't want any pity.

"I'm going to go get into more comfortable clothes anyway," Rachel commented to Natalia's back as she walked away. Her friends' eyes followed her until she disappeared into the dim light of the house.

Chapter 24

"Where are you going all dolled up?"

The rosy color on her cheeks turned a shade darker, the blush no longer needed from her makeup. The color crept down to her throat from Natalia's inquiring look. Rachel questioned if the sleek white halter dress was too much, but she assured her she looked stunning. Her friend gained enough confidence to give a little smile and twirl.

"If you must know... I'm going to dinner with Evelyn."

"Oh."

"You've been cleaning all day, haven't you?"

Natalia gave a light nod, her friend's point going over her head.

"The sun is starting to set. You know, you should get out sometime." Waving her arm towards the window. "Being cooped up all the time by yourself isn't going to help make your problems magically go away."

Stiffly, Natalia folded her arms over her chest. "Thank you, doctor. Anything else you'd like to diagnose?" Her tone dripping with sarcasm.

"No. I'll leave you alone." Rolling her eyes at the comment, she pushed her hair out of her face, dismissing her friend's mock tone.

"Besides, I don't want to be late."

Following her on her way out, Natalia handed over a spare key.

"We don't want you getting locked out." She smiled at Rachel.

"Unless you want me waking up the whole neighborhood again."

Both women giggled at the reminder of Rachel's past escapades. After a brief hug, Natalia stood on the porch, watching her friend make her way to her car and drive down the driveway.

About to head inside, Natalia heard another engine. A red Ford Explorer slowly made its way toward the house. Not recognizing the vehicle, she brushed it off as someone who must have been lost.

A low rumble as it came to a stop at the bottom of the steps. Recognition hit her, locking eyes with dark green ones when the familiar woman stepped out into the evening sun. The rays had her skin glowing.

Rubbing her eyes and blinking a few times to prove she wasn't seeing things. After all this time, Natalia couldn't believe she was here. Nick was really at her house, and she found herself speechless.

❧

Not sure she should be there in the first place; Nick froze next to the car. Expecting to see Natalia with another woman tore her to pieces inside, creating an urge to jump back in her car and speed down the road.

Instead, she found her alone and she couldn't take her eyes away from the beautiful vision on the porch. She looked amazing in a white shirt and dirty jeans. The sweat shimmering off her stuck to the patches of dirt.

Natural and pure look perfect on her.

"Hi."

The crack of her voice had heat rising to her cheeks. The attempt to clear the frog in her throat failed.

"I was around the corner showing another house, and I wanted to come by and see how you were doing."

Natalia's eyebrows raised.

"I- uh."

Oh, come on, Nick. Get it together.

"I mean... with the house. So how have things been?"

Anxiety grew as the silence stretched between them. Nervously, she ran her hands into her back pockets, rethinking coming over.

"I'm sorry. I shouldn't have come."

A knot filled the pit of her stomach, and she reached behind herself to pull the car door open again.

"I'll leave you alone."

Her fingers hesitated on the handle when she heard the one thing, she had been waiting to hear for weeks now.

Her voice.

"Why are you here?"

The wood beneath her feet creaked as she moved slightly. Swallowing, Nick dared to look up at her.

"And don't tell me you were just checking up on me. I don't believe you."

The words hard as she folded her arms over her chest.

Wow.

The anger lacing her tone caught her off guard.
She hadn't expected this much emotion.

What did you expect?

She asked herself, scanning Natalia's beautiful
eyes. Those eyes sparkled against the sun, and for a
moment, she wondered if she was seeing tears.

Did I cause that?

Standing here now, looking up at the woman
she loves and feeling like she does, she couldn't even
fathom why she waited so long to talk to her. Words
escaped her, playing hide and seek in her mind, and
she couldn't seem to catch onto one. Not wanting to
give excuses, she opted for honesty.

"I did want to see how you were. Although…
it - it isn't the only reason I came." Pulling her hands
from her pockets, she lifted them into the air as she
blurted out, " I missed you."

Her mouth parted, and her eyes widened.

" And needed to see you." Her words ended
with a plea.

Even from this distance, Nick could tell that
tears were starting to well up in Natalia's eyes. Natalia
covered her mouth with one hand and the other
wrapped around her middle.

Shifting her feet below her, an uncomfortable
realization that she may not be wanted churning in her
chest. She cleared her throat, her hands limp at her
sides.

Maybe I should just go.

Her shoulders slumped at the thought.
Confidence slowly dwindled inside her. Natalia's
hand dropped, and she wiped at her cheeks.

"So…" She said just above a whisper. "You came to see me because you feel guilty?"

Nick nodded.

"For not taking my calls or because you feel sorry for me?" The tone more solid and rising. Natalia took a step closer to the steps.

"I am - "

"Either way, you don't need to worry anymore." Tears spilled over, rolling down her cheeks. "I'm fine." Frantically, she tried to wipe them away, turning to go inside.

"Please don't go," Nick begged. Imploring her to stay and hear her out.

Stopping just inches from the front door, Natalia didn't bother turning around. She stood there, her back ridged as her hand stilled on the doorknob.

"I'm sorry it took me so long." Steadily, her words came out at a neutral pace – an enormous contrast to her nerves. "I really am. *Please* just listen."

Her pleas provoked no movement or acknowledgment. Natalia's rigorous focus on the door in front of her, coupled with her still form, showed an impliable stance. Nick's heart twisted as she continued her implore.

"I know I don't deserve your understanding."

Moving closer to the bottom of the steps. Her movements felt heavy, and her breath burned as she took in air.

"Or you, for what I have done, but I realized I can't function without you."

Her hand rested on the post at the base of the steps. The sigh gave her a moment to steady herself.

"I have tried the past few weeks, but I am driving everyone, especially my secretary, crazy because all I can do is talk about you."

Natalia's hair flicked to the side, accompanied by a soft sniffle. Unsure how to take that sign, Nick went on with her confession.

"I am so out of my comfort zone it is... it - it's scary. Sorry, I don't have another word for it. I wish I was better at this, but I am willing to fight for you."

Pushing off the post and straightening herself, she ran her hand across the back of her neck. Tension that had built up over this stressful situation caused an ache to form.

"When I saw you with that other woman, I didn't know what to do."

Natalia's shoulders froze, and her head snapped toward the door again. The deafening scream inside Nick's head made her sway for a moment. Natalia removed her hand from the doorknob and placed it on the frame, leaning forward. Still, she never turned around.

"I wanted to scream, but I decided that if she was what you wanted, then I could deal with it. I didn't want to get in the middle."

Dropping her head, Nick turned and walked back towards her car. Disheartened by the lack of response, she wiped a hand down her face.

"I can't get you out of my mind." She confessed. The truth came out fraying the edges of her protected heart, leaving her bare and vulnerable.

"That morning when I was shopping for you, I had every intention of surprising you and telling you – well, it doesn't matter. But, then, seeing you with that woman made my fears come to life."

You did say you would be honest...well, here it goes.

Pushing past her need to slide behind the wheel and flee, she trudged on, "I couldn't bear to get hurt again, and I didn't want to hurt you."

Unshed tears blurred her vision. With her heart wanting to beat out of her chest, she angrily wiped them away. Birds sang a happy tune up in the trees around them, and she wished she could join in their merriment.

Instead, I stand here while my heart is breaking. The corner of her mouth quirked up at the surreal situation she had placed herself in.

"I came here just to see you."

Melancholy as she opened her car door again. Her hand rested on the handle as she peered over at the woman she loved, still laying her head against the side of the door.

"Natalia, I couldn't take another second of... of whatever this is between us."

A shaky hand lifted, and Natalia rubbed at her arm. Nick's heart betrayed her with a flicker of hope, and she reprimanded it back into submission.

She still hasn't turned around and why would she? I don't blame her for being upset.

"Even just seeing your back makes my body ache to touch you."

Fighting back more tears, her voice came out hoarse. Clearing her throat did nothing to help it. For a second, she thought she might have heard her say something but brushed it off when nothing else happened.

"If I could live off of just looks, I would sustain life just drinking you in."

A faint noise, a mix between a whine and a whistle, floated to her from across the open space between them.

I didn't imagine that.

"If you tell me to go, then I will, and I won't come back."

"Nick." Came a whispering sigh.

"I could live without you, but I don't want to. Nat, I hate not being able to see you, talk to you, or be with you whenever I want to. I know what I want. What do you want?"

Saying her peace made her chest bitterly lighter. A weight lifted off of her with every sentence. Dread started to seep in as she waited for Natalia's answer. Her response would define what they were, and her impatience amplified because of it. Sometimes laying all her cards on the line left her worse off than if she kept her mouth closed.

Chapter 25

Not even bothering to turn around, "So what were you going to tell me the night you left the boxes?"

"What?"

"You said you had something to tell me. What was it?"

A cold sensation swept over her. Involuntarily, her hands rubbed at her arms. The importance of this question bumbled around at the back of her mind.

"Well?"

"I wanted to tell you - "

Natalia's hands stilled on her upper arms as an unease grew rapidly within her.

"I mean…I wanted you to know," The echo of the car door shutting reached her. "That from the moment I saw you, I felt a connection to you."

Her heart pounded in her chest. The blood rushing to her ears made it hard for her to hear what Nick said. Closing her eyes, she focused on the words.

"I never experienced anything like it before. It – you, caught me by surprise. That was what I was going to tell you,"

Natalia straightened and opened her eyes, preparing herself for what came next.

"That I love you."

Stunned. Speechless. Closing her eyes again, Natalia was at a loss, unable to trust what she had heard. The words.

Did she really just say that?

Those three little words that she had been dying to hear were finally presented to her. Spinning around caused her dizziness, and she almost tripped herself.

"Can you repeat that?" She had to see her say it. Needed to watch her mouth form the words.

Seeing is believing, they say.

Walking toward her, every step matching the rhythm of her heartbeat. Stopping at the bottom of the stairs, Nick looked up at her.

"I wanted you to know," Staring into her eyes, "I love you, Natalia."

The intimacy of their meeting eyes, the curve of her lip, had her audibly swallowing. She watched Nick's eyes fall to her throat. She followed the movement her jaw made when it clenched, and heat burned from deep in her belly.

Is it hot in here?

"And what about now?" Natalia persisted with her questions, "If you wanted me to know that then, what about now?"

Remembering the space created by all of this felt like an ice bucket being dumped on her libido.

"How do I know you won't just avoid me again? You just expect me to let everything go?" Nick's hand slid into her pockets. Her eyes remained on Natalia's.

"I am standing here spilling my heart out, telling you I am willing to fight for you. I wouldn't dream of avoiding you."

Nick bit back a curse as Natalia rolled her eyes. The low octave of her voice sent her heart racing.

"I don't have the strength to. I wanted to tell you then that I love you, but… I was getting in my own way."

Unable to deny that she had done that, too, Natalia remained silent.

Maybe we are more alike than I realized.

"I'm not letting myself do that anymore. I loved you then,"

Be still my heart.

"And I still love you now."

Her knees grew weak, and butterflies filled her stomach.

"I will keep loving you till the day I leave this world if you'll let me."

Oh my gosh, did she just say that?

Muffled thoughts under-shadowed her pounding heart. Cautiously, she made her way down the stairs, her legs growing increasingly unsteady the closer she got. Pacing herself, she mentally counted all six steps until she was face to face with Nick. A beaming smile greeted her and Nick reached for her hand. Squeezing it, she entwined their fingers.

"You know there never was another woman."
"What are you talking about?"

Nick's brows drew together and her smile was replaced with a frown.

"I saw you with her. You two were at a table." Nick released a blusterous breath.
Calmly, she replied. "You saw me with Dan."

Wrinkles formed across Nick's forehead. Natalia held back a laugh at her obvious confusion.

"I was breaking it off with her for the final time." She explained. "It takes forever to get through to her, although she was the one who did it to me first."

"The final time?" Nick questioned.

Natalia nodded. "I don't know why she just couldn't let it go."

"Oh."

Biting the inside of her cheek, Natalia stirred up the courage to wrap her arms around Nick's neck.

"I never got to thank you for my gifts." Her words were breathless against her hair.

"Oh, you don't have…"

Suddenly, Natalia kissed Nick forcefully, tipping her backward. They landed roughly against the side of the car. A moan escaped Nick as her hands slid up her back.

Nick's tongue pressed against her lips, and she opened, welcoming her in. The kiss gained feverish need as lips molded together like art sculpted from clay.

Groaning in protest when Nick pulled back. With a quavering voice, she replied, "You're welcome."

Natalia blushed at the devilish smile she received.

"So, I guess this means I'm forgiven?"

"You're mistaken if you think I'm that easy." Natalia teased, touching their foreheads together. "But I will let you know how you can work it off."

"Oh, I'll work it off, alright."

Leaning back, Nick kissed Natalia's forehead, before looking into her eyes again.

"I'm getting sweaty just thinking about it."

The innuendo had Natalia turning a dark shade of pink. Kissing this time, Nick wasted no time plunging her tongue deep into her mouth, and she swore Nick wanted her to swallow it. The connection sent electrical shocks up her spine, lighting fireworks off in her brain.

"I love you, Natalia Purez."

"My love for you is so inescapable, Nick Ward."

The sentiment reverberated around them as their mouths collided once more in heated unison.

∽

Nudging Nick back onto the bed after opening the curtains set off a colorful display to bathe both of them. Orange and purple smears filled the sky outside, pouring gleams of fire throughout the room as the sun set. Natalia backed up enough to be out of reach but close enough that she could see every feature, every fleeting emotion on the woman she loved face.

Nick couldn't hide her desire any more than she could hide the fierceness of her love for her. Clothes slipped onto the floor as Natalia stripped her top and bra off in front of her. Nick tried to sit up, to touch a sliver of skin showing itself, but she was met by a slender leg nudging her back with soft golden eyes telling her *not yet*. Giving up, she laid back on the bed, and a smirk played on her face.

Natalia began again. Her pulse quickened with every exposed inch. Licking her parched lips, Nick watched in awe, without interruption. The sight before her drew the breath from her lungs, leaving her speechless.

The orange and red glow from the falling sun spilled into the room, bathing the woman standing inches from her.

Goddess.

Natalia's skin burned everywhere Nick's eyes roamed, claiming every inch of her. The fire in her gaze caused a pool of heat to gather between her legs.

"Take off your clothes." Huskily, Natalia requested.

"But I'm enjoying my show." She answered with a smirk but inwardly groaned. "Besides, I can't go another second without touching you."

Sitting up with one outstretched hand, Nick pulled her to rest between her legs. The unbelievable sensation that the caress of the supple skin of her stomach made against her cheek was comforting.

Rubbing her face against her flesh was amazing, but she yearned more. Kissing her stomach, she made a trail up to her breast. Without touching the nipple, Nick leisurely kissed each one.

Natalia ran a hand through her hair, cradling her head to her chest. Softly, she whimpered every time Nick came close to her nipple and then retreated. Nick smiled against her skin and nipped at the sensitive underside.

Being very throughout, she made sure to kiss every inch. Satisfied that she didn't neglect either breast, she kissed the supple skin between them before leaning up and claiming her mouth once again. Natalia moaned into her mouth, deep and guttural, causing a primal need to overcome her, and she pulled her onto the bed.

"I want to taste every piece of you." She promised, licking her neck. "I'm going to make love to you so slowly and thoroughly," nipping her collar bone and eliciting a squeal from Natalia, "that you will never question my love for you ever again."

Taking her exhaled sigh as a submission, Nick rolled over, propping herself on top of her. Natalia gave in, enjoying every minute of attention. Nick palmed her breast. Filling each one with the heaviness. Her fingers clung to the tiny hard peaks and gently massaged them as she claimed her mouth once again.

Swallowing her moans, Nick loved the heat rising between Natalia's spread legs, taking the opportunity to grind herself against that sweet spot. Unable to resist, Nick sucked a hard pebble into her mouth, rolling it between her teeth.

Arching her back, Natalia pushed the hard tip further into her wanting mouth. Nick moaned against her sensitive nipple before sucking vigorously. Goosebumps sprinkled out over Natalia's smooth skin, and her hips jerked in response to another flick of her tongue.

"Fuck." A curse spilled past her lips, and Nick rubbed against her sweet spot once more. "Oh! Ah!"

Nick teased her nipples, switching between licking, sucking, and softly biting them. Natalia thrashed below her and rewarded her with the sweet scent of her dampness.

Finally releasing her nipple with a pop, she saw how swollen her breasts were as they rose and fell beneath her.

"God, you're beautiful."

Natalia went to protest but snapped her mouth shut when Nick rubbed against her again; Her words dying on a moan as Nick trailed kisses down her chest to her belly.

"Nick," Natalia's voice sang to her.

Natalia shivered beneath her, and Nick lifted her head to peer up at her. She had crossed her arms over her chest and giggled.

"What is it?"

"The wind." She motioned toward the window.

"Are you cold?"

A soft giggle again. "Not exactly."

Nick looked where her eyes had moved and noticed her nipples were sharp peaks glistening from her saliva. Prickles raised the skin around the peeks, and a sense of pride hit her.

"Oh," Her words were soft and knowing. Nick pulled her arms away. "I love seeing what I did to you."

"Fuck." She breathed low in her throat. Natalia's eyelashes lowered as she shivered again.

Grinning, Nick rubbed her cheek against the soft skin of her stomach before kissing it.

"Nick…"

Nick lifted her head and blew out a stream of air over each perky nipple. Her buds getting tighter, and Natalia squirmed underneath her. The whimpers she received made her clit throb and her lips tingle for more.

Ignoring her own need, Nick lowered her head again. Loving the scent of her, she breathed in a lung full of air through her nose. She wanted to bathe in her scent. As Nick's mouth reached her hips, Natalia grabbed at her shirt, fisting and twisting handfuls.

"I want to feel you against me. I need to!" She demanded. "Please, Nick."

Natalia's pleading words were like honey to her ears. Obeying, she allowed Natalia to remove her shirt. Intoxicated by their bare skin against one another, Nick's body hummed. Her need to consume her lover had her clit swelling, making her achingly sensitive.

Both women moaned in unison as Nick rubbed against her core again. At the brink of losing control of herself, Nick swore when her jeans rubbed across her clit.

"Nick…" Natalia panted. "Fuck, I might come."

"You can only come in my mouth."

Natalia groaned loudly. The sound produced more pre-cum to coat Nick's already slippery underwear.

"But – "

"Did you hear me?" Nick stilled, waiting for Natalia to confirm what she said.

Natalia whimpered and whined. She tried to get her to move again, but she stood her ground. When she realized she would have to wait, she bit her lip and nodded.

"Say it."

A whimper escaped her lips. "I hear you," she agreed.

Nick lifted onto her palms to look directly into her eyes. "What was that?"

Natalia rolled her eyes. She crossed her arms, and Nick looked back down at them, covering her chest. Natalia registered the tightness of Nick's jaw and dropped her arms to her sides again.

"Good." Nick praised. "Now, what was that?"

"I said, I hear you."

Nick leaned down and ran her tongue slowly around her taught nipple.

"Oh!"

"And...." She did the same to the other nipple, eliciting another moan. "What did you hear?"

"Come on!"

"Uh-huh."

Natalia huffed out air. With a pouty attitude, she responded. "I can only come in," Her cheeks blushed with pink, "your mouth."

"Good. Not so hard, was it?"

"Oh, you –"

Her words died in her throat as Nick sucked the whole nipple into her mouth.

"Oh! My! Nick!"

Natalia's back arched, and her hand gripped into Nick's hair, locking her mouth to her breast. Nick's moan vibrated over her breast, and Natalia moaned again.

"Nick.... Please...."

Nick's hand slid between them and cupped her sex over her jeans. Natalia jerked in response and gripped her hair tighter.

"Mmmmm...." Nick moaned and sucked as Natalia rocked back and forth against her hand.

"Nick.... I.... oh.... Nick!"

Sensing Natalia was close, she pulled her hand away. Natalia's grip loosened and she cried a protest as Nick released her nipple with a pop.

"I was so close."

Nick shook her head. "What did we just talk about?"

Cursing under her breath, Natalia laid back down against the mattress. Nick couldn't be mad at the adorable creature lying underneath her. Her damp skin from her mouth and blush color cheeks from panting made her all the more desirable.

Nick lowered her head and licked all the way down the crease between her breasts. Natalia covered her face with her hands and mumbled another curse. Nick chuckled against her skin.

"Someone is very impatient."

"Not my fault you took so long."

Nick chuckled again.

"Hey, it isn't funny."

"You're right." More serious now. "Making you come is serious business."

Natalia lifted onto her elbows and her mouth open wide, seeing Nick drop her head and lick all the way down her stomach, stopping at her pants. Warmth radiated from the woman below her, making electricity course through her body, creating a need to push her legs together to starve off her gush of wetness. Not able to, Nick inwardly groaned.

"I can smell you."

Nick commented unbuttoning her jeans. Natalia moaned at her words and moaned again when cool air touched her legs. Quickly, Nick peeled off her jeans and tossed them to the floor, returning back between her legs. She ran her nose up and down her thighs, feathering kisses as she went.

"Nick, I need – "

"Shhh."

Nick looked up and saw Natalia's round eyes pleading with her for more. She nipped the inside of her thigh, eliciting a yelp from Natalia.

"Hey!"

"Patience."

Natalia rolled her eyes and plopped back down against the bed.

Nick took the reprieve to see what she started. Her pink panties were soaked.

That is all for me, she praised herself. *I am so hungry.*

Pressing her nose to the fabric, she breathed in. A soft moan fed her ears, and she licked at the damp cloth. Natalia jerked beneath her and exhaled a loud moan. Curling her arms under her bottom, she slid her fingers into the waistband and roughly yanked the barrier away. Natalia squealed in surprise, and Nick tossed the underwear away. She lay between her lover's legs, staring at her prize.

"Perfect." She cooed, sliding back her folds, her fingers gliding through her moist center.

"Oh! Yes, Nick!" Natalia's hand wrapped around Nick's, urging her to continue.

"Baby," Nick warned, and Natalia dropped her hand. "I got this." She stated. "You just come for me."

Nick watched her nod her head and lay back down.

"I'm so hungry."

Growling, Nick dipped her head and sucked her clit in her mouth. A piercing scream filled the room, and a sharp jerk had Nick latching down onto the swollen nub.

Natalia whimpered, grinding hard into Nick's mouth. Nick sucked harder. Her hands wrapped around her thighs, pulling her meal closer to her greedy mouth as Natalia moaned and bucked beneath her. The sweetness filling her nose and mouth made her salivate, coating the sensitive nub in both their juices.

"Yes," she cooed, "Nick, right there." Natalia sucked in a breath. "Oh!"

Those words drove her even more. Nick's tongue stroked her clit in time with her bucking hips. The more intense her hips rocked, the more pressure she applied.

She tastes amazing!

"More Nick, please."

Her fingers dug into her hips and yanked her down hard against her mouth. The pressure had Natalia moaning out a scream. Releasing her hips, Nick slid her hands up and fondled her breasts. Rubbing and twirling around her nipples as she feasted on her swollen center.

"Yes!" She hissed out. "Oh my….Fuck.! Nick!"

Nick growled into her, vibrating her throbbing center. Hips jerked as Natalia fisted handfuls of sheets. Heat built between her legs as she slashed her head side to side, begging to come.

"Nick, I – I – I need to."

"Come for me, baby," she mumbled against the wetness. Loving every drop she gave her.

Climaxing on a scream, Nick felt her own clit twitch.

"Oh, Nick!"

Hips moved reverently when her orgasm broke. Nick's hands clamped onto her hips to hold her in place as she sucked everything she could from her.

Nick released her when she felt her muscles relax, and her breathing slowed.

"That… that…" She panted at the ceiling. "Amazing."

Exhilaration coursed through her veins when Natalia slid up and cupped her face.

"That was – you're amazing." She exclaimed, pressing their lips together.

"I have never felt anything like that. I'm so exhausted." She mumbled against her lips. "Can we just cuddle for a bit?"

"Sure, we can. Come here."

Easing over, Nick pulled the covers back, making a spot for her. She mumbled praises as she pulled her close and covered them both with the comforter. The glow of their lovemaking had Natalia smiling as a yawn came to her lips.

"Get some sleep." Nick fondly murmured into her ear. Kissing her head, Natalia snuggled into her warmth. Holding each other, their shared body heat eased them into a welcome sleep.

$\mathcal{C}$hapter 26

Her skin was still buzzing when her eyes cracked open a few hours later. The darkness outside sprinkled them with little specs of light. The humidity from earlier blanketed the room, leaving her in a cloak of sweat.

Turning, Natalia took in the woman lying peacefully beside her. Strands of hair in an array across her forehead, blooming a warmth within her chest. They had gone so long apart that it still gave her such joy to know they were finally where they were meant to be.

Memories of the night they shared flooded her while staring at her chest rise and fall. She wanted to relive the night through Nick's eyes, but she decided to do the next best thing. She could give back so gratefully what she had received.

Soft midnight shadows filled the room from the emblazoning moon as she eased down the covers and cautiously rose from the bed. Tip-toeing to her side, she prayed Nick would not wake. Exhaling a sigh of relief when she didn't, Natalia bent and timidly unbuttoned Nick's pants.

The beating of her heart drowned out the room as her fingers steadily tugged down the pants, along with her cotton underwear, revealing supple skin with just a kiss of tan. Her eyes devoured every inch of her well-toned muscular form as she dropped the vacant pants to the floor.

Having imagined this moment over and over again, Natalia questioned why she felt nervous. She craved the freedom to map out her lover's body but paused at the prospect of actually being able to do it.

Natalia's eyes traveled over soft curves, long legs, smooth muscles, and full lips. Drinking in every inch of her, remembering how perfectly their bodies fit together. Their frames designed for one another.

With nothing holding her back anymore and the demands of love exceeding the demands of life, her heart could no longer hide behind her insecurities. An overwhelming urge to touch her prevailed upon all of her senses.

Smiling down at the artistic vision in front of her, Natalia bit her lower lip before easing her body down on top of Nick's. Goosebumps broke out along her skin again at the skin-to-skin contact. Their joined bodies warm against one another.

Nick stirred slightly beneath her, causing warmth to pool between her thighs. Still, her eyes remained closed. Pressing herself to continue, Natalia released a shaky breath and lowered her lips to Nick's neck.

Kissing her way down, nipping at her collarbone, she stroked one of the hardened buds pressing against her chest between her fingers. A moan escaped Nick's lips, and Natalia felt bolder to go further.

Smiling to herself, she moved back up her neck to lightly suckle at her ear, making a tingling sensation pulse deep within her own belly.

"Mmmmm."

Drawing back, she looked into captivating foggy eyes. With a smile still playing on her lips, Natalia lowered her head and nuzzled their noses together before claiming her mouth. A warm rush of wetness greeted Natalia's thigh.

"Bab – "

"Don't speak," she whispered against their parted lips. "Don't say a word. I want to taste every part of you."

With determination steadily beating inside her, she persisted.

"You already heard my love for you." Her thigh gently rubbed between Nick's legs, spreading her juices along her skin.

"Mmmhmm."

" You've seen my submission to you last night." Natalia ran her tongue along Nick's bottom lip. "Now I want to play."

Lifting, Nick attempted to resume their kissing, but Natalia pressed the palm of her hand to her chest - over her beating heart - holding her against the bed. Nick mumbled in a half-sleepy state, but Natalia could not make out the words.

"I need you to fully understand how deep my love is, and the only way to do that is to – ."

Shifting her shoulder, Natalia was thrown off balance and tumbled forward with a gasp. Nick stopped her speech with a searing kiss. Nick was dominant and needy, invading her mouth with her greedy tongue. She moaned against her. Nick's hand reached between them, and Natalia broke their kiss, pushing her hand away.

"Turn over."

Nick's brows furrowed together, and the coy smile on her face contrasted the question in her eyes as she began to turn.

"No, on your side."

She instructed, and Nick nodded. Resting on her side, Nick faced away from her. Admiring the view with a few seconds of longing, she slid her body against her bare back. The building need between her legs surged again so she focused on the loving feeling of their shared body heat.

"Close your eyes."

Even though her words were soft, it was meant as an order. The light tone had her heartbeat picking up. Seconds passed until she was confident Nick had done what she asked. Muscles tensed as hands began caressing up Nick's arms to her shoulders. Fingers tracing the outline of her sides. Nick's bottom rocked backward, seeking for more.

Natalia chuckled low.

"Eye's closed." She reminded.

She touched almost everywhere, skipping over the extra sensitive areas. A small groan of impatience escaped Nick's lips, making Natalia smile.

"Shhh," she cooed against her ear.

Delicately running her fingers over her arms, she created more goosebumps. Easing her hand down between her breasts and over her stomach, Natalia nibbled on Nick's ear.

"Baby." The husky lull had Natalia squeezing her thighs together.

"Shhh." She reminded her, sliding her hand down to cradle her hip. She craved to dip her hand into the sweet spot between her legs, but her attention to detail had her holding back. She didn't want to rush this. Five minutes passed of repeating until Nick was a squirming mess in her palms.

A sharp intake of air broke the silence as her tongue and mouth moved feather-light kisses down her neck. The waiting was validated with the persistent rubbing of Nick's ass into her belly. Nick's small pleas for her to touch all the parts that she was trying to avoid, Natalia caved and moved her hand up to tease a nipple.

The tip of one finger rolled and flicked at her nipple. Arching her back, Nick attempted to make more contact, but she kept backing her hand away.

"Baby…"

Natalia was surprised with how much restraint she possessed while her sex was weeping with unspent need.

"Not yet."

Images of rolling her nipple around in her mouth conjured more cream to settle between her folds. Her mouth watered at the insatiable appetite those images created. She swore she could almost taste the flavor of her pink rosebud skin against her tongue.

Giving herself completely, without rules or complaints, ascended an adrenaline rush she had never felt before. Natalia couldn't fathom why this beautiful woman could possibly want her. Having nothing to offer in return except her heart and soul, she decided she would give them to her fully without inhibition. Vowing silently that there would be no limitations to her love for this woman in her arms.

Releasing her hold on her nipple, Natalia maneuvered her hand down over her stomach even further to cup her warmth. Frustrated, Nick grabbed her hand, pressing her palm firmly against her sex. She screamed out her pleas, needing release.

"You're not abiding by the rules."

Inside Natalia was grinning as she tugged Nick to lay onto her back. Surprised, Nick just blinked up at her.

I am stunned that this strong woman is so easily moved, she admitted to herself. The power it made her feel aroused her, gaining more bravado.

"Now you'll have to suffer."

Her strict tone softened with a devious smile. Watching as Nick visibly relaxes into the mattress.

Dipping her head, she lapped at each nipple like they were saucers of milk, intentionally making licking noises. Nick arched her back at every lap, frustrated and needing more pressure for longer. She growled deep in her chest and reached for Natalia's head to press her down onto her but stopped when their eyes met.

Natalia left her craving more, making disapproving noises, and she prided herself on such control. With a whimper, she briefly gave in and suckled each little pebble into her warm mouth. Nick cried out sounds of satisfaction and gratitude.

Suddenly, Natalia released her nipples and slinked down the length of her without taking the time to tease. Nick gripped the sheets of the bed and released a frustrated moan.

"Come on." She complained to the ceiling.

Natalia grinned and reveled in the feelings it brought. Settling between her legs, she stared at the shimmering folds of her sex, as if inviting her. Not wanting to be rude, she lowered her head and suckled the swollen clit into her greedy mouth.

The cries were a welcome treat to her ears as she devoured Nick's sweet softness. A firm hand tangled in her hair as her hips bucked. Moving to encompass her swollen folds, Natalia ravaged every portion of her. The sweet scent of her cream filled every fiber, every pore of her existence.

"Baby. Yes....Yes... You're so good. Oh!"

Only when Nick's body began to tremble did Natalia shift her mouth back up to suckle on her clit. Thighs shook as she slipped two fingers inside her tight center. Applying more pressure, Natalia gave Nick's swollen bud a nip.

"Fuck!"

Crying out, Nick bucked her sex into Natalia's rapacious mouth, resulting in her fingers dipping up to her knuckles. Sweat glistened off Nick. Small beads grew as she climaxed. The awe-inspiring sounds pushed her on to suckle harder. Back arching off the bed, Natalia gripped around her thighs and rode out her climax with her.

After she had drained every last drop of sweet nectar from her tense body, Nick collapsed. Pulling herself up to lay beside her, Natalia basked in her partner's afterglow. The shallow rise and fall of Nick's chest made pride bloom inside her.

I brought this incredible woman crumbling down into a sedated mess.

"Oh. Wow." Nick panted. Her eyes fell shut once again, and Natalia knew she was spent. Settling next to her, she pulled a blanket over the top of them.

"Get some sleep, my love.", kissing her forehead.

Nick had already drifted off. Her breathing was shallow, and her lips parted. Smiling, Natalia rested her head against her arm and closed her own eyes.

How did I get so lucky? She wondered. Praying that this peace never has to end.

Chapter 27

"You two are so cute together," Rachel commented while opening a can of soda.

The fizz was partially muffled by her voice. Continuing, "I thought you'd never get up this morning."

The sly smirk made Natalia roll her eyes at her friend.

"Seriously though, I'm so happy for you, Nat. You look rested for a change." Taking a swig from the green can, Natalia's eye watched her friend's throat bob. Temporarily distracted from the gulping.

Clearing her throat, Natalia shook her head and half-heartedly laughed at her friend, who just burped.

"Thank you for getting everything ready for the party Rachel."

Rachel nodded in acknowledgment. Her eyes scanned the area around them.

"I had a nice long night, and I needed it too."

"What's going on?", she asked, leaning in.

"What," Natalia retorted, backing away a step.

"You're glowing. What's going on?"

The mischievous smile her friend produced had heat surging to her face. Rachel wiggled her eyebrows, a tell-tale sign she suspected something.

Sighing, "Nick is the one. I can just feel it."

"Well, she better be."

The smirk never left her friend's face. Straightening, she picked a piece of hair from her shirt.

"I don't need any more meltdowns."

Both women stared blankly at each other for a brief moment before busting out in laughter.

"Speaking of the one, here she comes now." Rachel tilted her head.

Looking over her shoulder, Natalia's eyes pinned onto the woman walking toward her. Water dripped down off her hair, leaving damp areas on her shoulder.

I can't believe I am jealous of a shower.

Admiring the image coming towards her, a warmth grew deep inside her the closer she came. The smell of tangy sweetness greeted her senses.

"Hi, sexy."

A soft kiss caressed her lips in a welcoming greeting.

"I brought some extra clothes with me this time," she mumbled against her lips. The seductive tone had chills running through her. Pulling back, "I hear Fletcher is bringing Jake over to say thanks. He wants to meet the doctor that went to the edge to save his best friend."

Realizing Rachel was in the room, Nick shifted to face her. "Hey Rach. How are things going?"

"Could be worse."

"I heard about the big move. If you want, I have some listings in the car. You can take a look."

Rachel let out a laugh, shaking her head. "You never stop working, do you?"

Nick threw up her hands and shrugged, making Natalia smile.

"You two go ahead. I'm gonna start the grill."

Mouth opening to protest, Rachel waved her hands.

"People will be here soon, and I want to make sure I have the food ready. Besides, you both will just get in the way."

Lightly chuckling, Nick put an arm around Natalia.

"You sure? You don't want any help?"

With a shake of her head, she waved her away.

"No, I don't need any help. I can handle it."

Nick gently tugged on Natalia, who kept looking over her shoulder. A worried expression played on her face.

"I've got this." Trying to assure her as she was pulled away, "Besides, Evelyn will be here soon, right? You should go look around before she gets here."

Natalia paused, which caused Nick to stop. The arm around her still lightly nudging.

Placing a hand on her hip, Rachel looks at Nick. "I don't want you wasting your attention on papers instead of your girl."

A knowing smile and nod from Nick. "Agreed."

Rolling her eyes, Natalia gave into being led away when Rachel winked at both women.

"Oh, okay," she conceded.

Waving the two women off, she said, "I'll meet you out there in a minute."

Reaching the front door, Natalia stopped and flicked her hair over her shoulder, "So what was all that about?"

"Nothing."

A squeal sounded.

Did she just pinch my butt?

The coy smile confirmed it.

"Stop it."

"I don't want to." Kissing her exposed neck.

Natalia rolled her eyes and straightened her clothes.

"If Jake's coming, I need to find something resembling dog food."

"Oh, I can do that," replying with a light kiss on the cheek, "You just take care of the party...for now."

A smack filled the air, followed by a light stinging from Nick's hand on her bottom. Natalia let out another soft cry.

"Was that a hidden meaning?" She asked, rubbing her backside.

"Oh, you can take a hint, can't you?" Nick teased, accompanied by a wink. "Well, don't waste all your time out here. I want a piece of you too."

Nick ran her tongue over Natalia's lips, sealing her message. Her insides heated up at the inclination burning within Nick's eyes.

Her words were thick and husky, "You won't get just a piece, you'll have the whole thing,"

Grabbing around, Nick pinched Natalia's rear and greeted her again with a squeak. A contagious smile spread over Nick's face.

"I love you and your cute butt too."

She rubbed the spot she had grabbed, tightening her arm around her and pressing their bodies together. Her insides burned, and heat crept up her throat.

"This is prime real estate, by the way. I need to do a thorough walk-through."

Stunning Natalia, speechless, Nick kissed her cheek and released her grip, turned, and left to go in search of dog food. Natalia stood in the doorway, mouth agape. Moments passed while she watched Nick gain distance between them before blinking.

"I love you too!" Calling out as loud as she could.

Epilogue

Two years of dating Nick turned out to be the best two years of her life. Their souls were completely in sync with one another, leading her to believe that soulmates were real. Never once did she have to try to love her, or try to be something that she wasn't. It all came naturally and Natalia wondered what made her steer away from this woman in the first place. Truly happy and in love for once in her life.

Still, at the peak of their relationship, Nick decided to sell her apartment to move in with her. Figuring she was always at her house anyway, it didn't make much sense to pay for a place she was never in.

The move took Natalia by surprise, but she had no complaints. Wanting nothing more than to spend the rest of her time with the woman who bought residence within her heart. In a matter of a week, they would be together full-time.

Rachel wasted no time. Within three weeks, and with the help of Evelyn, Rachel found her little slice of the countryside. Just last month, Rachel had a commitment ceremony showing the world and her long-time friend she had found the woman of her dreams. A resilient woman who wasn't afraid to settle down and tame the wild mustang inside her. Natalia couldn't be prouder of her.

Starting this fall, Natalia and Rachel will be going back to work part-time at the local ASPCA to lend a hand. Deciding that they needed the time off but couldn't deny the call of animals in need. The idea excited her and she looked forward to getting her hands dirty again.

Speaking of dirty, Natalia started a small farmette after purchasing a thoroughbred gelding and two pygmy goats just last year. On a whim, she also purchased a dozen hens to add to the farm. Feeling fulfilled taking care of the animals, only a small slice of her cake.

She loved watching Nick's reaction to the different animals too. Taking pride in going and collecting the eggs from the hen house every day, calling the basket, she carried her 'collection plate.' A feeling of contentment filled her as she spoke softly to the mother hens, plucking their eggs from their nest.

Gracie sent people by the house if they needed help with their animals. Making sure to always call first after one farmer heard certain loud noises coming from an upstairs window.

Natalia's face burned bright red for a whole week after. It became a nice little side business to help pay for the house. Next year, Nick promised to trim her hours at the agency and make more time at home.

The wind whipped at her cheeks as she remembered the delightfully long conversation of wanting to have the sound of little pitter-pattering feet running around. She had looked into adoption, but the only way either of them would agree to it was if they both had enough time at home to raise a child.

It goes to show, she thought, *that no matter what life would throw at them, they knew if they both relied on each other and trusted one another, they would always have one another. Money doesn't always buy happiness*, she told herself, staring at her lover sitting in the rocking chair, *but in this case, it did help to gain some prime real estate.*

The End

Look for more books on www.gt@publishing.com or anywhere books are sold online. My Rayne Falls Ranch series is out and ready for a read! Don't forget to jump into this series. The third installment coming soon! You can also grab some of my merch on SpreadShop or type in the link below!

https://gt-publishing.myspreadshop.com/sinful+grace?collection=VudpecnRQN

Thank you for reading.

Remember,

"You can't have History, without a Story in it!"

Sinful Grace